Oliver Hassenca

Shiver...
The Shiverstone Boys
Meet the Rose Cliffs
Girls

Translated by Dieter Morgans
With illustrations by Silvia Cristoph

RANDOM HOUSE PTY LTD

Random House Australia Pty Ltd
20 Alfred Street, Milsons Point, NSW 2061
http://www.randomhouse.com.au

Sydney   New York   Toronto
London   Auckland   Johannesburg

First published in Australia by Random House Australia 2004
Original title: *Auf Schreckenstein geht's lustig zu* by Oliver Hassencamp
© 2000 by Omnibus Taschenbuch/C. Bertelsmann Jugendbuch Verlag
a division of Veerlagsgruppe Random House GmbH, München, Germany

National Library of Australia
Cataloguing-in-Publication Entry

Hassencamp, Oliver.
The Shiverstone boys meet the Rose Cliffs girls.

For children aged 10+.
ISBN 0 7593 2083 7.

1. Boarding school students – Juvenile fiction. I. Title.
(Series: Hassencamp, Oliver. Shiverstone Castle; 2).

833.914

Cover and internal illustrations by Silvia Christoph
Cover design by Jobi Murphy
Typeset in 11 on 15pt Palatino by Midland Typesetters
Printed and bound by Griffin Press, Netley, South Australia

10 9 8 7 6 5 4 3 2 1

Contents

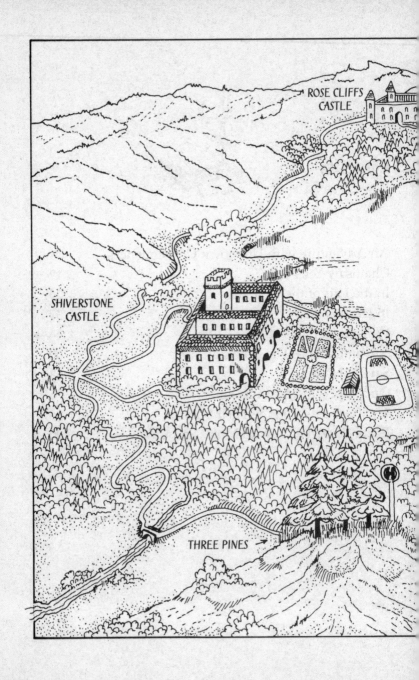

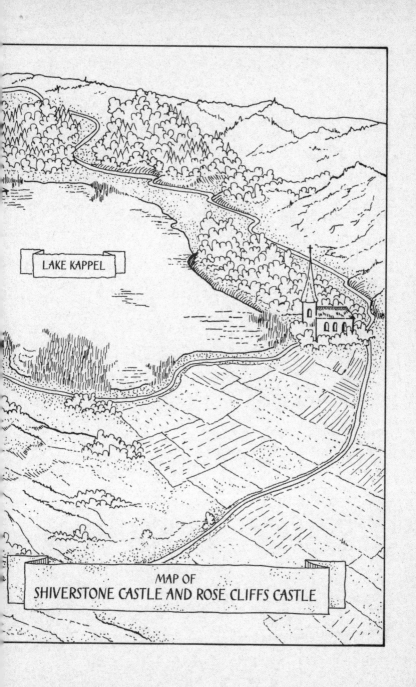

LAKE KAPPEL

MAP OF
SHIVERSTONE CASTLE AND ROSE CLIFFS CASTLE

An Adventure with Unknown Consequences

The school at Shiverstone Castle was already a year old. Moving into an old castle where knights had once lived had initially only been an emergency measure due to the lack of room in the old school building, but things had worked out so well that the change was made permanent. The boys had changed a lot since moving into the castle! In the old days, if anyone had refused to cheat or copy someone else's work, the rest of the school would have thought that they were a little bit thick, but after moving to Shiverstone none of the students ever cheated, even when they had the opportunity. Exactly why their behaviour had changed so dramatically, no one could say. The most popular theory was that it had something to do with the castle. The boys had become just like the knights who had lived at Shiverstone in the past. As a result they were always honest and fair. They always took responsibility for their behaviour. They even took responsibility when they misbehaved!

1

The kid they called Bulldozer was still the strongest and the biggest of them all, but he no longer held the shot-put record, not since the new pupil, Steven Brewer, had arrived. At first Steven had seemed like a typical showoff with an electric guitar and the latest stereo equipment – a music system so powerful it could hold hundreds of hours of music, but so small that it fit in your shirt pocket. But there was more to Steven than that, and soon he became one of the most respected knights in the castle. His closest friend was Otto, who was constantly beating his own record as the best eater in the school. Otto's current record was twenty-three pieces of apple cake with cream. Steven and Otto made a great pair. Steven was the one who had the ideas and Otto was practical, putting the ideas into action.

Otto and Steven had been invited to their history teacher, Mister Waldmann's, birthday party. It was pretty special to be invited to a teacher's party, but the three of them had been through a lot in the last year, so it was only natural the boys would be invited. Even though Mister Waldmann, Otto, Steven and Sonya, Mister Waldmann's daughter, were an odd combination, they were really good friends. The four of them had worked together to stop the school from being closed down and turned into a casino, and their friendship had become even stronger since that adventure.

Otto was enjoying himself at the party. After he'd cut himself his sixth piece of cream cake and eaten it, he set his plate down and said, 'Yes, those were the days!' as though their school-rescuing adventure had happened more than twenty years ago. Without waiting for a response from the others he cut himself another piece of cake.

'You like the cake, huh?' teased Sonya, but Otto didn't react.

'I have to eat or my teeth'll get bored,' he calmly replied.

'What are you doing with yourself these days, Sonya?' asked Steven. Sonya had lost her job as a singer in the bar called The Green Owl when Clink, her old boss, had failed in his plans to turn Shiverstone from a school into a casino. After his scheme failed, Clink soon ran out of money and had to close down The Green Owl.

'I've got a job as a music teacher,' Sonya said.

'What kind of music?'

'All kinds. Modern stuff and classical music. The job's at a girls' school.'

'A *girls'* school?' Steven grimaced.

'As a matter of fact the school is directly opposite Shiverstone. It's on the other side of Lake Kappel.'

'A girls' school across the lake from us? You're joking!' Otto looked at her in astonishment.

Mister Waldmann looked at his watch. 'Goodness, it's already ten o'clock! We've certainly talked away the evening.' He turned to Sonya. 'How are you getting home?' he asked.

'I don't actually know,' she replied sheepishly. 'The last bus went at 8.15.'

Steven and Otto looked at one another. They both had the same idea. 'We'll paddle you across,' they said at the same time.

'That's great! Thanks guys!' Sonya looked relieved. 'I'd completely forgotten that the school has a new fleet of canoes.' She looked questioningly at her father.

'That sounds fine,' he nodded. Letting the boys out on the lake at night was a huge vote of trust in them. 'But don't do anything stupid, and come straight back. Otherwise I can't guarantee what Rex will say.' Rex was the school's principal.

'You can rely on us!' Steven replied and stood up.

Sonya kissed her father goodbye.

'Thanks for the cake!' the boys said as they stealthily made their way down to the boatshed. Otto untied a canoe and Steven helped Sonya step into it.

'You're both real gentlemen,' Sonya remarked as the boys cast off and the boat cut through the coal-black water.

The two boys were quiet as they paddled. Sonya was already twenty-five, and usually girls her age had nothing in common with boys their age, but Sonya was an exception to the rule. She was friendly, courageous, quick-witted and always ready for some fun. The boys sometimes had trouble keeping up with her.

'How you two aim to get across the lake in this pitch blackness is a mystery to me,' Sonya said after a while. 'I would have turned back ages ago.'

It was so dark that you couldn't see your hand in front of your eyes, but Steven and Otto were both experienced with the canoes and Lake Kappel. If they paddled perfectly in time with each other, like they'd done time and time again at paddling practice, the canoe shot forward as straight as an arrow. Steven was

4

right-handed and always pulled a little to the left. Otto was left-handed and pulled to the right. The two boys balanced each other out. They had launched the canoe parallel to the jetty. There were no currents on the lake to pull them off course. Nothing could go wrong. Still, the longer the journey took, the spookier it became.

'If only we had a torch,' Sonya blurted out, starting to get nervous.

'You want to wake the fish, do you?' Steven asked. 'Of course we've got a torch, but if we turn it on now we'll only paddle in circles.'

'What if we crash? There's cliffs on the other side.'

Steven wasn't worried. 'It takes 4,763 strokes to get across the lake, and we've only done . . .'

'2,491 . . . 2,492,' Otto counted out loud.

Sonya calmed down. The boys seemed to know what they were doing. Each of them fell quiet, wrapped in their own thoughts. Mister Waldmann either had a great deal of trust in these two or no experience whatsoever in nightly canoeing trips.

On the 4,750th stroke the air became cooler. The smell of pine trees surrounded them. Otto and Steven brought their paddles in and turned on the torch.

It was so quiet you could have heard a mouse walking over the grass. Like the trail of a ghostly gown, the torch-light stretched across the darkened water. Gradually the shadowy outline of the coast began to emerge.

'There!' Sonya called out. 'I know where we are now! Turn right and head that way another 50 metres, then you can land the boat under the willows.'

Steven and Otto followed her directions. The branches of the weeping willows hung right down to the water. They had to part them like curtains to slip underneath. Suddenly a good sized bay opened out. There was even a boatshed with a pier. Otto was amazed.

'Man, that would be the perfect harbour for us!' he said.

They moored beside the pier and Sonya jumped out.

'How long have you been living at this girls' castle?' Otto asked as he tied up the canoe.

'Ssssh! Not so loud!' Sonya hissed. 'You'll wake everyone! You can go now. I know my way from here.'

'No.' Steven caught hold of her wrist. 'You said we were gentlemen. We're taking you all the way.'

Sonya shrugged. When Steven and Otto got an idea in their heads it was usually best to play along. If you said no, they'd do what they wanted anyway. The boys walked on either side of Sonya as they climbed the steep path that lead from the pier into the forest. Sonya was happy to indulge them in their games of chivalry. She understood that the chance to get a closer look at her school, Rose Cliffs Castle, was too good an opportunity for Steven and Otto to pass up.

'At least turn off the torch!' Sonya hissed. She'd suddenly become very nervous.

The three of them moved quietly through the trees until the ground evened out, and they came into a clearing.

'Thank you, boys. I can definitely take it from here,' Sonya whispered hurriedly and was suddenly gone, leaving the two boys standing.

6

'Hm,' Otto grumbled after a while. 'Now that we're here . . .'

'It would please Mister Waldmann no end if we took a closer look at the architecture of this castle. After all, he is our history teacher.' Steven finished Otto's sentence for him.

'Absolutely right,' Otto agreed.

Rose Cliffs Castle seemed to be smaller than Shiverstone Castle. It was a square design, two storeys high, with a tower on every corner. It's from the Renaissance period, Steven thought to himself, an observation that would have pleased Mister Waldmann. But at that precise moment Mister Waldmann was asleep on the other side of the lake. In fact, everyone was asleep – at Shiverstone and at Rose Cliffs too. If Otto and Steven had bothered to listen they would have heard heavy, rhythmic breathing coming from the opened windows.

Next to the main building was a second, smaller building – a kind of shed. Steven dug his elbow into Otto's ribs and the two boys headed towards it. Suddenly there was a dull thud, and Steven rubbed his shin.

Otto shone a thin stream of light through the fingers of the hand he had cupped over the front of the torch to see what Steven had tripped on. He started to chuckle.

'Will you look at that,' he whispered. Across the path lay a ladder.

'It's a personal invitation to climb inside,' Steven whispered back, grinning.

The two boys burst out laughing so loudly that they had to clamp their hands over their mouths until the hooting subsided. Once they had calmed down they started looking for a suitable window. They found one around the side of the building and leaned the ladder up underneath it. Steven began to climb, carefully holding his breath and inching himself up one rung at a time. Before he got to the window he stopped once more to listen. He heard the rumble of a deep, loud snore coming from inside. That can't be a girl, he thought to himself, the excitement of the discovery making his knees knock. Turning, he quickly made his way down the ladder again.

'Back already?' Otto asked.

'There's someone in there, snoring like a walrus!'

Hastily they removed the ladder and ran around the corner. From where they stood they could see a long, dark shadow rising up against the shed wall. Steven pointed in its direction, and Otto cautiously approached it.

'It's only a wood heap,' he said. 'Now it's my turn!' They set the ladder up on the new side of the building, resting it carefully underneath an open window.

Otto climbed up this time. Steven held the two sides of the ladder to steady it. The silence was so profound that Steven started to get a bit spooked. Finally a soft 'Pssssst!' came from above. The coast was clear. Wasting no time, Steven climbed up and found Otto standing in the middle of a room in front of a table, shining his torch onto a piece of paper that he held in his hand.

'It's a classroom,' he said without looking up. 'Here!' He handed Steven an exercise book.

Steven took the book and looked through it. It was almost full, written – he thought – in a typically girlish script, all squiggles and flourishes. Otto walked over to the open window and sat on the windowsill.

'Check it out,' said Steven. 'Five out of five, four out of five, four and half . . . seems to me you've got a lot in common with this, this . . .' He closed the book and read the name on the cover. ' . . . this Beatrix Lebkowitz.'

'What do we do now?' asked Otto. 'It seems a shame to just head back home now that we're here.'

The two boys leaned out of the window and gave the matter some serious consideration. Steven tossed the torch from hand to hand as he thought, until it suddenly fell out of his grip and landed with a dull thud on the woodpile underneath. Unfortunately it had turned itself on when it landed. Luckily it was facing the wall, and only shone a small circle of light back against the ladder.

'Idiot!' Otto hissed. The two boys froze, holding their breaths and listening for any sound that might reveal they had been discovered. After a few painful minutes Steven climbed down to switch the torch off. He had to inch across onto the wood heap, which was quite high. It was made of thin pine branches all stacked together, each of about a metre in length. They were all oozing sticky pine sap. Eventually he managed to snag the torch. As he did he had an amazing idea. It was so amazing, he didn't worry about the fact that he'd dropped the torch again.

Tucking one of the pine branches under his arm, he shimmied back up the ladder.

'What do you want with that stupid piece of wood?' Otto asked.

Steven wasn't listening. 'I'm going to try something.'

He carefully swung himself into the room and turned the torch on. Walking softly so that the floorboards wouldn't creak, he made his way to the door. He lay the piece of wood on the ground, and began to take measurements. Yes, his plan would work. The piece of pine was slightly taller than the door handle. If he slid it under the handle, and secured it on the floor with a chair or a desk, no one would be able to open the door from the passage outside.

As quickly and noiselessly as he could, he returned to the window and climbed down.

'Grab a bunch of branches,' he ordered. 'We're blockading all the classroom doors.'

The plan was carried out in no time. Otto and Steven carried the ladder from window to window. One boy would climb up while the other grabbed the next branch. In a few minutes all eight classrooms were barricaded, and could only be opened by climbing through the windows and unlocking from the inside.

With the confidence of sleepwalkers on familiar ground the two boys found their way back to the pier where they'd moored. They were so pleased about their successful scheme that it only took them 4,702 strokes to reach their home pier.

'Well, finally!' A gruff voice cut through the darkness.

'I was starting to get worried!' It was Mister Waldmann. He stood on the pier, his teeth chattering. He hadn't been asleep in bed after all!

'Everything's fine,' Steven said, trying to avoid a direct question about why they had taken so long.

Mister Waldmann ignored the boys' cheeriness and cut to the chase. 'What took you so long?' he asked. 'It's two o'clock in the morning!'

'We're glad we found our way back at all in this dark,' said Otto. 'We didn't get to see any of the scenery.'

'There's no time for chit-chat!' scolded Mister Waldmann. 'Off to bed with the two of you! And be quiet so that Rex . . . ah, Principal Meyer doesn't catch you!'

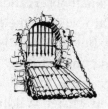

Chainsaw Yells 'Fire!'

'You celebrated for ages last night,' said Walter, the youngest in the room, when Steven and Otto could barely crawl out of bed next morning.

'You should have been asleep and not up waiting for us,' Steven replied.

Apart from that small observation, everything went well. Steven and Otto weren't the most awake in the classroom that day, but they hardly ever were, so no one noticed anything unusual.

They were only wide awake once during their history lesson, when Mister Waldmann told them of the naval battle at Salamis, in the Aegean Sea, when the Greek navy soundly defeated the Persians in 480 BC.

'It's still unclear how the Greeks navigated their tiny ships without any instruments and managed to remain on course, even at night,' said Mister Waldmann.

'You old Greek, you . . .' Steven whispered to his friend.

Water seemed to be the theme of the day. After lunch Rex declared, 'There's no sport this afternoon.

Our landlord, Count Shiverstone, wants us to organise a school fire brigade in case there's ever a fire. He's lending us his water-pump, and he's coming to the training exercises himself.'

Resounding laughter broke out.

'What's so funny about that?' Rex said, even though he was trying hard not to laugh himself.

The fire drill with Count Shiverstone as Captain was all everyone could talk about. They assembled after lunch in the courtyard. Everyone had been told to wear heavy shoes.

'There they are,' said Walter suddenly, holding his hand in front of his mouth. Everyone glanced in the direction Walter had pointed and quickly had to find something to stuff into their mouth to stifle their own laughter. Rex walked up to them wearing gumboots and a leather jacket, which was funny enough, but it was Count Shiverstone whose appearance bowled them over. He wore a long oiled raincoat that was far too big for him, and a giant floppy hat that was pushed way down his forehead. All that was visible was his bulbous nose. The Count had stuffed his feet into lace-up boots that looked as though they had been around for hundreds of years, and he carried a walking stick with a silver knob at the end of it.

'Good day, boys!' shouted the Count in a brisk tone. The boys, still swallowing their giggles, responded to the call with an energetic, 'Morning, boss!'

Rex pretended that he had lost something important on the ground in front of him so that the Count couldn't see the big smile on his face.

The Count was startled by the unexpectedly energetic greeting, but he recovered quickly. His speech was laced with growls and grumbles as he continually cleared his throat. Whenever he spoke he grumbled so much that he sounded like a chainsaw, which was what the boys all called him.

'You all know why we . . . hrrrrr . . . why . . . hrrrrumph! . . . why we're here,' Chainsaw stuttered. 'During this drill I'll need . . . hrrr . . . four strong boys . . . khrrrrrr . . . to man the pump . . . Steven, Otto, Walter and you,' he said, pointing at Bulldozer, and motioning the four boys to follow him. Pulling a huge iron key out of his pocket, he strode towards the castle gate.

'Oh dear.' The words escaped Steven's lips before he could stop them when Chainsaw pulled back the heavy gate to reveal their 'fire engine' sparkling in the afternoon sun. Though it was clean and shiny, it was obvious to all of the boys that their fire engine was a genuine antique. A large metal cylinder with a hose coming out of it sat on a wooden wagon. At the opposite end was a second hose that ended in a sort of suction device. Sitting on top of the cylinder was a long iron lever. The whole contraption was incredibly strange looking. The boys weren't convinced that it would work at all.

'This piece of equipment,' began Chainsaw, indicating the ancient pump, 'was built to the specifications of my great great great . . . hrrrr . . . great grandfather . . . in the year seventeen hundred and . . . hrrr . . . something or other . . . and has saved this castle three . . . hrrr . . . three times.'

'He's a pretty good tour guide,' Otto said, commenting on the Count's speech.

With everyone's help the pump was pushed into the park. The wooden cart groaned under the weight of the pump as it rumbled over the cobblestoned courtyard. The Count had decided the drill should be on his side of the castle, which was something he'd soon regret!

The boys were organised into various battalions, each with a teacher as 'commander'.

Mister Stemmer, the Geography teacher, was put in charge of the 'water battalion', whose job was to take the long snaky hose with the suction device attached and race down to the lake with it, dangling it into the water so that the pump could be filled with water.

Mister Rolle, the Sports teacher, was in charge of the 'demolition battalion', who had the dangerous job of advancing towards the 'fire' with raised pickaxes, in order to pull down anything that was in the way of the stream of water.

Mister Blume, the Music teacher, was in charge of the 'rescue battalion', who were responsible for the rescue of personnel and household goods.

Mister Waldmann was in charge of the 'gardeners battalion', whose task was to fling heaps of sand onto the smaller outbreaks of fire.

Bulldozer, Otto and Steven were the 'pump battalion'. Bulldozer's job was to turn on the tap that sent water through the hose, while Steven and Otto were given the job of working the main lever that sucked water from the lake and sent it through the hose towards the fire.

The use of the hose itself was allocated to either Chainsaw or Principal Rex – no one else.

Once all the jobs had been allocated and everyone stood at their post, Chainsaw made his announcement. 'I'm going inside to . . . hhhrrrrr . . . set off the fire alarm. As soon as . . . hrrrrr . . . as soon as you hear it, you all start performing your . . . hrrrrump! . . . your allocated tasks!'

'I think he might need that raincoat by the time the drill is through,' said Claus, who was the biggest joker of the whole school.

'Don't be too enthusiastic. It's not a real fire this time,' Rex said.

'Fire!' called a voice from inside the castle. 'Fire!'

'Fire!' Rex called down the line, gesturing to the battalions to start working.

'Sorry, I don't have a light,' said Claus. Rex ignored him.

The water battalion raced down to the lake, preparing to dunk the hose end.

'Don't dunk it yet!' said Mister Waldmann as he watched the gardeners battalion throwing sand into the carefully tended rose beds. 'We don't know where the flames are coming from yet!'

'*What* flames?' asked Mosquito.

'That's right,' said Mister Waldmann. 'It's only a drill, so we only pretend to do what we're supposed to.'

'Supposed to what?' persisted Mosquito.

'Supposed to fight a fire!' snapped Mister Waldmann.

17

Everyone started pretending to throw sand by waving their shovels in the air, laughing all the while. Rolle had similar difficulties convincing the demolition troop to take things seriously.

'It's in!' yelled Strehlau, the head of the water battalion, dropping the suction pump into the lake. Steven and Otto began working at the pump's lever.

'Nothing's happening,' said Bulldozer, turning the tap on and off and on and off in frustration.

Chainsaw, who had been standing stock-still at his window, began to get restless.

'What's the problem? Where's the . . . hrrrrrr . . . where's the water? I would have been burnt to a . . . hrrr . . . to a cinder by now!' he yelled, as loudly as his rusty vocal cords would let him.

'It's coming!' Steven called up to him, and then as a joke, added, 'It just takes time for Bulldozer to work things out! He'll get it right soon!'

'You'll keep!' hissed Bulldozer. He had no sense of humour when it came to jokes about his intelligence, because he knew that he wasn't particularly smart.

'Chill out, Bulldozer – we're only mucking around,' grumbled Otto, but he could tell that Steven's comment had started up the old feud between the two of them.

A sudden thumping from the Count's window made everyone turn around. A couple of the students had taken it upon themselves to rescue the household goods by leaning a ladder against the wall and sliding all of the tables and chairs down it.

'Are you mad?!' screamed Mister Blume as he ran off to stop them.

A loud hissing started coming from the water pump as its tank began to fill with water.

'Get ready, Bulldozer!' Otto called out.

Chainsaw still stood at his window. Steven and Otto kept on pumping the lever with all their might. The nozzle of the hose gave a gurgle, but the sound of the water rushing into the tank was so loud that Bulldozer hadn't heard Otto's warning. He turned around, still pointing the hose at the Count's window.

'What did you say?' he yelled.

The hose gave a sudden jerk and a jet of water shot out and hit the Count square in the chest. It swept him off his feet like a tidal wave. Oblivious, Steven and Otto continued pumping the lever.

'Drop the hose!' Rex repeated in a thunderous voice. Bulldozer, as slow to take things in as Steven had said, turned his head and frowned at Rex, still pointing the hose straight at Chainsaw's window.

'What?' he screamed at Rex.

Despite all the noise and confusion, Steven had managed to hear what Rex had said.

'Stop, Otto!' he yelled. The two boys stopped pumping and the water pressure began to subside. Steven was about to tap Bulldozer on the shoulder when the sound of breaking glass came from inside the castle. Jean, Chainsaw's butler, had tried to close the window to shut out the water. The jet of water had proven too powerful, however, and the window pane had shattered into pieces. With the pumping stopped, the jet became a spray and finally just a dribble as the damp disaster finally came to an end.

The knights had never seen Rex as furious as he was now. Sputtering, and soaked to the skin, he screamed at Bulldozer.

'Next time we'll give that job to the smartest student, not the strongest!'

'I didn't know when the water would come!' Bulldozer said, with an innocent expression on his face.

'You didn't KNOW?!' Rex yelled at him again. 'You should have!' He turned to face the other students, who had all gathered around the pump for a better look at Chainsaw's window.

'We'll talk about this tonight!' Rex said. 'For now the drill is over!'

That night, at the special assembly, the events of the afternoon were discussed in detail. Of course Rex couldn't really blame anyone, not even Bulldozer, whose only crime was that he had been slow to react. Even so, he decided a punishment was necessary, since the drill had caused a fair bit of damage.

'I give you as much freedom as it's possible to give any school. I don't care how many pranks you come up with – I won't punish even the cheekiest of them – *as long as no one gets hurt and nothing gets damaged*. But if there *is* damage – whether it's deliberate, or whether it's because you're being stupid or thoughtless – it will *not* be tolerated!'

The gardeners had buried about a dozen rose bushes. The Count's window had been broken. The jet of water had damaged the Count's inner rooms. Several table and chair legs had snapped off on their journey down the ladder. That didn't even take into account the shock the poor Count himself had suffered.

No one had meant to do it, that was clear. The problem was that no one had taken any notice of what they were actually supposed to be doing. The poor organisation and lack of concentration might well have been caused by Chainsaw's comical get-up, but that was no excuse.

'Over the next fourteen days,' Rex said, ending his lecture, 'no one will do any sport. Instead you'll all work in the veggie patch. I believe Heini would appreciate your help digging up the new crop of potatoes. And while you're doing that, please give a thought to what on Earth we're going to do to get the Count to forgive us! I don't think an apology will do the trick. We'll have to think of a more impressive gesture than that.' So saying, Rex left the room, and the school assembly was over.

A few days later, after the students were all sick of the sight of potatoes, Sonya paddled across the lake for a visit. She was impressed with the level of gardening expertise everyone had developed. Since she had helped to rescue the school the year before, she was universally loved and welcomed by the boys.

'May I present Madame with this small token of my esteem?' Mosquito asked, bowing and handing her a huge clump of dirt, inside which was hidden a tiny potato. Everyone rolled on the floor with laughter.

The boys told Sonya about the circumstances leading up to their forced labour. In turn she told everyone about her new teaching position, because of course Otto and Steven had kept it a secret so that their pranks would not be blamed on them.

'What?! There's a girls' school over there?' asked Hans doubtfully.

'You bet there is,' said Mosquito, giving a superior little laugh.

'How would you know?' Dieter asked.

'I'm good at geography. Anyway, my sister goes there,' Mosquito replied.

'What? And you only tell us now?' hissed Bulldozer.

Mosquito immediately bit back. 'Since when have you and I ever discussed girls? Anyway, you've got your own sister, haven't you?'

That ended the conversation. Steven and Otto had wisely kept out of it. It was only after the digging, when they stood alone at the pier, that they carefully asked Sonya about the fruits of their nightly venture.

'How's it been your side of the lake, lately? Did you get back inside all right?' Otto asked with the most innocent expression in the world.

'I was lucky no one caught me,' she replied. 'But the strangest thing happened the next morning.' She went on to tell them what had happened. Otto and Steven had to work hard to look surprised and not laugh too loudly or too soon.

'Our school janitor had to climb into every class-room and take away those pieces of wood,' Sonya finished off.

'That idea's almost too good for a girl,' Steven cheekily thought out loud. Otto shot a warning glance at him. He didn't want Steven to give the game away.

Sonya had no idea the two boys were responsible. And even if she had suspected, she would have dismissed the suspicion immediately, considering how dark it had been, and how unfamiliar the school grounds would have been to the two of them.

'Don't underestimate what girls can do,' she said seriously. 'The two girls who were caught have to peel potatoes every day as punishment.'

'What do you mean "the two girls who were caught"?' Steven's surprise nearly let the cat out of the bag.

'Oh,' said Sonya, 'they haven't admitted it, but everyone knows they're the culprits.'

'Potatoes always seem to be the punishment,' Otto complained, rejoining the conversation. 'I think it was a really good prank! It should be rewarded, not punished!'

'Just between the three of us, I think so too,' said Sonya. 'But our Principal isn't like Rex.'

Steven and Otto nodded silently.

'Anyway, I've got to go see my father, and then I have to get back before it gets dark. It takes me over 5000 strokes – and that takes time,' she laughed, and left them. The boys watched her go.

'She counted the strokes! How cool is that?' said Otto.

Steven didn't reply. He was busy thinking. Eventually he spoke up.' What do you think about this prank business?' he asked.

'Hm? Oh. Not much, I have to say,' Otto replied.

Steven nodded. 'It was a terrific prank, without doubt. But to let two innocent parties take the rap – that's no good.'

'Even if they are girls,' said Otto.

'Should we tell her when she comes back?' asked Steven.

'Sonya? No! Things like this shouldn't be handled by a go-between. I don't think Sonya would let us come back with her anyway.'

'And we have to go back, that's for certain.'

That's what they were like, these Shiverstone boys. They aimed higher and achieved a lot more than any city kids in city schools. They had something not many others their age had: backbone. They had a strong sense of what was right and what was wrong. None of their teachers had drummed it into them. They'd come up with these principles themselves simply by living in a genuine knights' castle. They had even come up with a motto:

As long as I am at Shiverstone
I will be true to everyone.

The motto made it crystal clear what Otto and Steven had to do.

24

In the Lair of the Leopard

Steven and Otto wanted to apologise to the girls who'd been blamed for their prank, but they weren't sure when and how they would do it. It had to be soon so that the innocent parties could stop suffering. Mornings were out, because they had class. Afternoons might be alright – they didn't have sport at the moment, but they'd have to find a good excuse to get out of digging potatoes. The chance to get away from potatoes made the two boys try hard to come up with something. It had to be a really good excuse. It wasn't that they had to convince Rex – they could have told him the truth about why they needed to go and he would have let them. It was because of the other boys. If they found out that Otto and Steven were going to own up to the prank, that would have been okay – it was in keeping with their beliefs as knights to own up to the things you'd done. But if they had found out that the boys were going to go to a girls' school they would have teased them for the rest of their time at Shiverstone. Steven and Otto wanted to avoid that at all costs.

As usual, Otto came up with a bright idea. 'Didn't Rex say we had to think of something that would be a gesture of apology to Chainsaw?' he asked.

'Yeah, so?' Steven mumbled suspiciously.

'I know what'll make him happy! He's a birdwatcher, right? Why don't we build him a hide in the forest so he can watch the birds without being seen himself?'

'Hey!' Steven said, punching Otto in the chest; 'That's a great idea! If we build a hide in the forest we can disappear every afternoon!'

It *was* a great idea, because Chainsaw's land curved around almost two-thirds of the border of the lake. The boys would be able to openly launch their canoe and no one would question them.

'Not a bad idea at all,' said Rex when they told him their plan. 'You can start immediately.' And with an understanding smile, he added, 'Of course you won't be able to work in the veggie patch. I hope that's okay with you two.'

Five minutes later the two boys were running to the boatshed armed with an axe and a saw.

'Where are you two off to?' asked Mosquito, who had wandered over with a bunch of other knights to see what the fuss was.

'We have to harvest the underwater potatoes. Rex's orders,' said Otto and ran off.

When they reached the other side of the lake, every-thing was quiet. They snuck in under cover of the willows and looked across at the pier. There wasn't a soul in sight. Without saying a word they tied up the canoe and climbed the steep path into the woods. The closer they came to the clearing the more nervous they felt. At the edge of the clearing they carefully peered through the last branches. There wasn't a girl to be seen anywhere. Quietly they walked up to the castle. In the daylight sun the rosy glow of its stonework made it clear why it had been called Rose Cliffs Castle. Beside the left-hand tower an old man was working with a hoe. He had his back to them.

'Let's ask him,' suggested Otto. Steven nodded.

'Hello there,' said Steven, approaching the man. 'We were wondering if . . .'

The man turned and measured them with a surly look. 'What do you want?' he growled.

Steven was stuck. He didn't know the Principal's name. Otto stepped in to rescue Steven before the game was given away.

'We're here to see Miss Waldmann,' he quickly said.

The old man straightened up and almost smiled. 'Aha, Miss Waldmann,' he said. 'Well, follow me.'

He put the hoe down and walked ahead of them. Steven and Otto looked at each other, relieved, and followed. The first hurdle had been overcome. There still wasn't a girl in sight, and so they took the opportunity to check the school out in daylight. They walked past the shed with the ladder. Beside it was the woodpile, and right above it the classrooms.

Steven suddenly had the feeling they were being watched. Slowly he turned around. Peering out of one of the windows in the second floor were five girls, watching them with interest. When they saw that he had seen them, they ducked quickly out of sight.

The old man turned a corner around the tower, and they came to the entrance.

'I take it you have a message for Miss Waldmann from her father?' their guide asked as they walked up a wooden staircase.

Think quick, Otto, thought Otto to himself, and replied, 'Yes, we've come from Mister Waldmann.' It wasn't *exactly* a lie.

'Ah!' said the old man and laughed. 'That means you belong to those notorious Shiverstone boys.'

And so saying he opened a glass door and stepped into a long passageway. Along the right hand wall were windows overlooking the courtyard. Along the left hand wall was a row of doors. Between the doorways stood rows of lockers, just like they were arranged back at Shiverstone. One of the doors opened and a tall, blonde girl came out. As soon as she saw them, she stopped, and stepped back through the door she had entered through.

'Here we are!' The old man knocked on a door. 'Miss Waldmann, you have visitors!'

'Come in!' a voice called out from inside the room.

Steven mumbled thanks to their guide and the two of them went in.

Sonya sat at a desk in front of a window. When she saw who her visitors were she stared at them as though they'd come from Mars.

'You can't just turn up here whenever you want!' she gasped.

'Oh,' replied Otto, much calmer now that he was among friends. 'We just wanted to visit you.'

It didn't sound very convincing. Sonya eyed them suspiciously and, after a few false starts, they broke down and told her the truth.

Sonya chewed her lip thoughtfully. 'You've put me into a tricky situation. The old lady – I mean Principal Horn – can't under any circumstances find out that you two brought me across the lake in a canoe.'

'Yes, but . . .' Steven began.

Sonya cut him off energetically. 'Under *no* circumstances! I'm the youngest teacher here and still under probation. Anyway, she's already biased against me.'

Now it was Otto's turn. 'But Sonya, two innocent girls were punished for something they didn't do. We don't want that on our conscience.'

'All right. Well, I can bring those two here and you can apologise, but that's all you can do!'

'But Sonya,' Steven tried again. 'We don't just want to apologise. We don't want them to be punished any more.'

Sonya wasn't convinced. 'You promised my father you'd take the canoe back immediately. But you didn't, did you? And now you want to pull me into this mess as well! The answer is no.' She turned her back on the boys and stared out the window.

Otto shrugged his shoulders. Then, slowly and thoughtfully, Steven said, 'Sonya, you know yourself how we think at Shiverstone. If anyone does something wrong they have to own up to it. You agree with that, don't you?'

'Well, yes,' said Sonya without turning around.

Steven continued. 'The two of us were responsible for the prank, and you got home late. All three of us have to own up to what we've done.'

Otto quietly gave Steven the thumbs-up signal. He was convinced that Sonya would take the bait. But it took a while, before she replied.

'Okay, alright, you've made your point!' she said finally, sighing. 'Otto and Steven, you're impossible to argue with!'

They discussed how best to break the news to Principal Horn. Sonya had done a complete turnaround. She wanted to come with the boys when they apologised. Before they'd really come to any conclusions about who should speak first they were standing in front of the door to which was attached a brass plate that said:

Principal Adele Horn.

Steven raked his fingers through his hair one last time. Otto tucked his shirt in. Sonya took a deep breath and knocked.

'Come in,' rasped a hard voice from inside.

Sonya entered. She mumbled an apology for this unexpected interruption and introduced the boys. Principal Horn was a thin woman with an almost vulture-like head. She stared at the boys with her severe, green eyes.

She looks like Chainsaw's sister, Steven thought to himself. He looked around the room. The walls were full of shelves containing books. He was just examining what kind of books they were when Principal Horn spoke to him.

'So you're from Shiverstone, are you? Then you must be here because you've done something wrong,' she said.

Steven gave himself a mental nudge to calm himself down. 'Yes, Principal Horn,' he began. 'We're the ones who barricaded those classrooms and we want to . . .'

'You mean to say you snuck around these grounds in the middle of the night?' interrupted Principal Horn. 'That is the height of cheek!'

Steven tried to continue, but Sonya took over.

'Otto and Steven brought me over in their canoe after my father's birthday celebrations. Unfortunately I'd missed the last bus.'

'You paddled across the lake? At night? Who gave you permission to do that?'

'It was the best solution we could come up with . . .' Otto whispered softly.

Principal Horn sat up straight in her chair. 'Best solution? Is this an example of the things they teach you over there? I can't say I think much of the education they're giving you!'

She scolded them so harshly and spoke so quickly that they could hardly follow what she said. They could tell, however, that nothing she said about Rex was a compliment. The three of them stood there as though a summer storm had suddenly overtaken them in an open field.

After Principal Horn had finished, Steven started to speak.

'We know we'll be punished for what we've done. We don't want to talk our way out of it. We only came

32

because we'd heard that two innocent girls had been punished for our prank, and we don't think that's right.'

Principal Horn hadn't expected such fair minded-ness. Her eyes wide, she stared at Sonya, then levelled her gaze at Steven and finally turned to Otto, who felt like he had to say something.

'That's right,' he said, meekly

'Fetch the girls,' said the Principal to Sonya. While Sonya was out of the room doing as she was bid, the two boys were measured silently by the Principal's steely gaze. Finally Sonya returned with the girls.

Steven recognised the taller girl with the blond mop-top. She was the girl he'd seen in the hallway. The Principal introduced them. 'This is Beatrix,' she said, indicating the taller girl. 'And this is Ingrid,' she said, nodding towards the shorter girl. She had dark hair and looked a lot like Mosquito, which was no surprise since she was his sister.

The two knights also remembered that it was Beatrix's exercise book they'd found in the first class-room – Beatrix was the girl with the excellent marks.

Without raising their heads, or giving either of the boys a single glance, the girls listened to their confes-sion. As soon as the knights had finished Principal Horn sent them out again. And after several more warnings that such a thing would never happen again as long as she was Principal of this school, the lecture was over.

'And next time you can catch the bus!' she said sternly to Sonya before she looked away and began fussing with something on her desk. 'You are dismissed.'

'She's a nightmare!' Otto muttered once they were back outside in the hallway.

'Now you know why I wasn't so keen in the first place,' said Sonya.

'Well, at least she reacted sensibly when we told her the truth,' said Steven.

'I suppose,' said Sonya. 'Now. I think I can detect a certain tension in the air. I'd better escort you two back to your boat.'

She was right. The place didn't feel very friendly at all. Girls were staring at them from behind every cupboard, every door, and every corner. None of them were staring in a curious, or even friendly way. The boys had to run the gauntlet. On the stairs leading outside they met a round woman with friendly eyes. She smiled at Steven and Otto as they passed. 'Boys at Rose Cliffs? How about that!' she said.

'That was Mrs Buckle. She teaches Geography and English,' said Sonya.

'She's the first friendly face we've seen since we arrived,' said Otto.

Sonya hurried the boys out of the school grounds and over to the edge of the forest. She looked agitated and worried.

'I have to go back now. When you see my father, can you let him know that I may need his help?' And so saying she bid them goodbye and quickly left.

'Poor Sonya,' said Otto as he watched her go.

Steven nodded. 'Sometimes the truth gets you in trouble.'

'But at least you can sleep with a clear conscience,' said Otto. He was grinning. They'd overcome the worst. But they hadn't overcome the worst at all, not by a long shot. The worst was yet to come. Their first indication of the trouble they had started for themselves came when they returned to the pier. Their canoe had been filled to the brim with water and was completely submerged!

'Well, that's just great!' grumbled Steven, taking off his shoes and socks. The two boys waded out knee-deep into the lake so that they could lift the heavy canoe onto land in order to empty it. The hardest part of the job wasn't how heavy the canoe was. It was the fact that as they lugged the canoe onto dry land they were pelted from every side by taunts and insults and cat-calls coming from the trees.

There were girls hidden everywhere. They watched and laughed and made fun of Otto and Steven's efforts. When the boys tried to swing the canoe up onto the shore, a hundred voices started calling out 'Heave! Ho! HEAVE! HO!' and burst into laughter when the canoe tipped back into the lake.

'Shut your traps!' Otto yelled angrily into the forest. The only response this brought was a long, drawn out 'Boooooo!'

After nearly half an hour of emptying the canoe they were finally ready to push off. They had barely started paddling when a huge crowd of girls ran at them from all sides, screaming at them and teasing them even more as they attempted to escape.

'Let's get out of here!' gasped Steven and started paddling so hard that the canoe groaned.

The inlet that connected the bay to the main body of the lake was barely five metres across. The crowd of girls ran towards it to cut Steven and Otto off. The race was on. The boys paddled for all they were worth. As they approached the branches that hung down to the water, they stopped paddling and ducked their heads. The girls had got there first and were splashing water from both sides as they continued their screaming taunts.

Finally the canoe reached the main body of the lake. The two boys glanced up. They both looked as though they'd had a shower with their clothes on. The floor of the canoe was ankle-deep in water again. They watched, stunned, as Beatrix ran into the lake, stopping only when the water reached waist-hight. As they paddled away she shouted after them.

'Next time you come to visit, make an appointment, you cowards!!'

Steven stood up, nearly capsizing the canoe, and yelled back, his face red with anger.

'Shut your face, you witch!'

And with that the horrible episode finally came to an end.

In Harm's Way

Despite being soaked and exhausted, Steven and Otto still had to find a position for the hide on the way back to school. They pulled into shore at the first suitable spot they could find. They stripped down to their bathers, leaving their soaked clothes to dry in the sun, and headed inland.

Steven's father was a birdwatcher himself, so Steven had a good idea about the kind of thing to look for when building a hide.

'How much further to go?' Otto finally asked, dragging the long saw behind him.

'I'm looking for nests,' Steven replied.

They found a small clearing surrounded by a circle of medium-sized trees, and Steven began peering up into the branches for any sign of bird nests.

'Here!' he called suddenly, and pointed up at a nest sitting halfway along a thick branch at the top of the tree. 'And there, and there,' he said, pointing out several nests, 'and there's a hollow tree, a cuckoo would use that for sure.'

They walked away from the clearing, back among the trees, and found one that had a fork in its branches about three metres up.

'That's where we can build the hide,' Steven explained. 'Chainsaw will get an excellent view from up there.'

They marked the spot and the path that led to it by making notches in the trunks of the trees they passed as they walked back to the lake. On the shore they built a small stone pyramid so that they could see the landing place clearly when they were on the lake. Their clothes had dried in the meantime, so they dressed themselves and paddled home. They were quiet on the return journey. They just couldn't understand the girls' reaction. They'd confessed to their misdeeds, hadn't they? The innocent were no longer being punished, right? So what was going on? Why were the girls so annoyed with them?

Steven was particularly upset that Beatrix had called him a coward. He'd never been called a coward before in his life. He didn't like the way it made him feel at all.

Otto sat at the front of the canoe. He was responsible for keeping them on course, so he just stared straight ahead, into the water, saying nothing. They were so pre-occupied that they didn't realise someone was waiting for them until they were just about to moor. It was Rex, watching them with a stony expression.

A submarine would be handy right about now, Steven thought to himself.

'We've found a great spot for the hide, Principal Meyer,' Otto said, being as polite and formal as possible.

'And I've had a great phone call,' Rex said in a clipped voice. 'You two. Come with me.'

Steven and Otto ducked their heads in shame, but no matter how slowly and carefully they tied up the canoe, it couldn't save them from the inevitable. They were in disgrace and they had to follow.

'I expected better from you two! To think you trespassed in a girls' school!' Rex scolded them as they walked up the path.

Behind a corner of the boatshed stood a grinning figure. It was Bulldozer. Judging by his expression, he had heard everything, and was hugely amused by Steven and Otto's embarrassment.

Mister Waldmann was waiting for them in Rex's office. He gave the boys a glance as cold as Rex's, wordlessly shaking his head. Rex sat down at his desk and lit his pipe. The two boys remained standing.

Maybe smoking his pipe will relax him, thought Steven. Rex didn't say anything until he had finished the entire pipe. The silence in the room was unbearable. Eventually he laid the pipe down and spoke.

'Principal Horn gave me a call this afternoon. You've put this school into a difficult position. But before I say what I think, I'd like to hear your side of the story.'

Otto began by avoiding the question.

'We went over to Rose Cliffs so we could apologise to Principal Horn, and then we started work on the hide for the Count.'

'No one's questioning your work on the hide. But you haven't answered my question,' said Rex, deflecting Otto's avoidance strategy.

Steven grew very calm. It was his turn to speak. He had to explain the situation on his own. No one could beat Otto when it came to working out a tricky technical problem, but when it came to using a bit of diplomacy, Steven was the one you turned to. Their combination of practical and theoretical talents was why the two friends worked so well as a team.

'We made two mistakes,' Steven began. 'First of all, we climbed into those classrooms, and secondly, we didn't tell Mister Waldmann immediately.'

'If it was only as simple as that!' Rex interrupted him. 'You've brought the entire school into question!' He started to walk up and down the office. 'You know perfectly well that I allow you far more freedom than any other school would. If there are problems, we deal with them ourselves! But if you abuse this freedom – if you behave badly outside the school grounds – then *I'm* blamed. Which means I will have to be stricter in future.'

Mister Waldmann tried to take part of the blame onto his shoulders. 'I shouldn't have let them go,' he said.

'Of course you should have!' countered Rex. 'You weren't to know that two of our knights – especially these two – would abuse your trust in such a flagrant manner!'

Mister Waldmann looked visibly shaken. 'Why didn't you tell me?' he asked the boys.

'I don't know,' Otto said, shrugging his shoulders. 'You sent us straight to bed when we arrived back and the next day, well, we just didn't get around to it. We missed our opportunity.'

'We didn't want any of the others to find out about it,' Steven said, 'so we didn't tell you either. Which was a stupid thing to do.'

'Why didn't you want the others to find out about it?' Rex asked.

Steven spoke uncertainly, his voice becoming soft. 'We . . . we thought they'd laugh at us.'

Rex sat down again, to relight his pipe. 'Well, they know now, and I'm sure they'll let you know they know!'

'We've been stupid,' Steven said through gritted teeth.

It seemed as though Rex had been waiting for this admission. His voice became calmer and friendlier. 'Yes, you have, but I suppose things like this happen from time to time. Principal Horn certainly had a lot of criticisms about the school, but your apology seems to have impressed her more than she's ready to admit.'

He paused, and smiled at them. 'You'll have to deal with the other knights yourselves,' he said. 'As far as I'm concerned, the whole thing's forgotten. In fact, I thought the prank itself was quite funny. So let's say nothing more on the matter.' With that he stood and motioned for the boys to leave. The boys were so amazed by Rex's conclusion that they left without saying a word.

Rex had been right. Bulldozer had done a good job digging up the dirt on Otto and Steven, and an even better job spreading it! Wherever the two boys went they were laughed at, and ridiculed.

41

'If you like the girls' school so much, why don't you two transfer there?'

'You'd look cute in a pinafore, Otto!'

'Look, here come the Rose Cliffs knights!'

'Pink really suits them, don't you think?'

It was a relief for the two beleaguered knights to paddle away from the teasing and potato-digging activities and work on their building project, even if they were teased about that as well.

'Sneaking back to the girls' school, are we?'

'Hurry! You don't want to be late for cooking class!'

'Don't forget to bring your sewing needles, boys!'

They avoided the others whenever they could. They even kept to themselves in the evenings. Steven practised his guitar and Otto, who didn't play a musical instrument, sat nearby and listened. One evening he was tapping along with Steven's playing. Steven immediately had an idea.

'Hey, you don't have bad rhythm at all! Why don't you join the band as our drummer? We're getting sick of the sound of the drum machine on Strehlau's keyboard. There's a drum kit in the music room that you could borrow!'

Otto got permission from Mister Beuscher to use the music room for drum kit practice twice a week. The rest of the band was glad for Otto to join, even Strehlau, who had to admit that he didn't really like the sound of the keyboard's drum beat either. And so a new talent was discovered. Steven and Otto's humiliation had at least one happy outcome – the school band, Excalibur, expanded its lineup. Steven played guitar,

Hans was on vocals, Strehlau played keyboard, Mister Rolle played bass guitar, and Otto became the drummer. But despite the good news on the school band front, the boys continued to tease Otto and Steven.

'Is it true that you want to be just like Kylie Minogue when you grow up, Otto?'

'You two should go over to Rose Cliffs and form an all-girl band!'

'This is all because of those stupid girls!' Otto grumbled in annoyance.

'Forget about it,' Steven calmed him. 'They'll get bored eventually and stop teasing us. In the meantime there's one thing I know for certain. I'm going to get even with that Beatrix Whatshername! You just wait and see!'

Whispered Plans at Rose Cliffs

Beatrix felt the same way about Steven. She might have forgiven him for the four days of potato peeling she had to do because she'd been blamed for his prank. At least he'd owned up to that. What she couldn't forgive him for was that he'd called her a 'witch'! How dare he? She'd get him back for that!

Beatrix and Ingrid, Mosquito's little sister, were the same kind of people as Steven and Otto. They were always up to something. Principal Horn was quick to catch and punish anyone who misbehaved, so most of the girls at Rose Cliffs were always on their best behaviour. Not Beatrix and Ingrid! They were the only ones who had dared to pull pranks at Rose Cliffs. They were responsible for the mouse that had turned up in the Maths teacher's bed. When the mouse jumped into the poor woman's hair as she pulled back the covers one night, she almost fainted! Since that incident, anything that was remotely naughty or out of order was Beatrix and Ingrid's doing.

The strict way Principal Horn ran the school meant

that good relationships between students and teachers couldn't develop. Because the teachers were always making sure that the girls behaved, the girls could never properly trust their teachers the way the knights at Shiverstone could. Right from the start, everything was simply forbidden.

There was one person the girls could trust, though. Someone who they could talk to about anything at all. Someone who would much rather have been their friend than an authoritative figure. That person was their Music teacher: Sonya. She'd been able to win the girls' respect in a very short time by being understanding instead of being strict.

Because of her father, and also because of her friendship with Steven and Otto, Sonya had a much more modern attitude towards teaching. This made her much more popular with the students than any other teacher at Rose Cliffs. Sonya admired people who knew what they wanted, who knew their own minds, and who took risks if necessary. So of course she admired Ingrid and Beatrix.

Ingrid and Beatrix were known as the 'wild ones' among the teachers. There was always something going on with those two. Beatrix had an acoustic guitar, her 'axe', as she called it, which she could play really well. Ingrid had a quick mind just like her brother and was a talented comedian. In the evenings she would often impersonate the teachers for the rest of the girls, who would be in stitches when she started up her comedy routines.

Beatrix was trying to think of an interesting enough plan for revenge on Steven. One evening she asked

45

Sonya what life at Shiverstone was like. Sonya knew exactly what she was up to.

'Is that Rex person really generous when it comes to clever pranks?' she asked.

'Yes, he is. He loves a good prank as long as nobody or nothing gets hurt or damaged,' said Sonya.

'So he wouldn't call Principal Horn and tell on us if we . . . ooops!' The cat was out of the bag now.

'You're not planning revenge on Shiverstone?' Sonya asked, sternly.

'We are!' Beatrix and Ingrid replied. 'And we want you to help us!'

'No. No way. That's totally out of the question,' Sonya said.

Saying no to Beatrix only got her excited. 'We can't let those two types just wander in here whenever they like!' she said. 'Our reputation's at stake! That Steven kid called me a "witch"!'

'Be sensible, Beatrix,' Sonya tried to calm her down. 'If Principal Horn finds out you'll be in so much trouble.'

'How's she going to find out if their principal doesn't tell her? Anyway, no one would ever expect us to do anything like this! All we want to do is paddle over and then turn their school on its head.'

'Yes! What they can do, we can do a thousand times better,' Ingrid said, adding to Beatrix's argument.

The two of them told Sonya what they had planned in such detail that even she was tempted to play a part in their plan. She knew that if she said no, the girls would go ahead anyway. Better to be part of the prank so that she could minimise the damage caused, she reasoned. She decided to pretend to disapprove for a little bit more, then make a big show of being convinced by the girls.

'I don't think so, girls. I don't see why I should help you pull a prank on Shiverstone. My father is a teacher over there and those boys are my friends.'

Ingrid became insistent. 'And now you're a teacher here, and you're *our* friend.'

'You are,' Beatrix underlined that fact. 'We women have to stick together.'

Sonya pretended to give in. 'All right,' she said. 'I'll help you, but under one condition. *I* determine what happens over there, and we won't let too many people in on the prank.'

'Of course! So you're in? Excellent!' Beatrix was unstoppable now. The thought of taking revenge on Steven gave her such a high that she jumped into the air for joy.

They worked their plan out to the smallest detail. Three other girls – Renate, Eva and Sophie – would come along with them. Those three girls were as reliable as they were secretive.

In case their disappearance was noticed, they decided to say that they had gone on a midnight swim. They'd already done that once and were only lightly punished for it. And now, with a teacher supervising, there was less chance of being punished. They hoped.

A couple of nights later the six of them were paddling across the lake in the starlight. They wore jeans, woollen jumpers and soft-soled shoes. They carried one torch each and a very long piece of rope. Fearlessly they glided their canoes into the Shiverstone jetty, figuring that amongst all the other canoes, theirs wouldn't be noticed.

Shiverstone castle lay hunched into the hillside like a sleeping bear. Sonya led the way up to the castle. At this time of night there was no danger of meeting anyone. She remembered that Otto had told her that the front door of the castle made loud creaking sounds, like Bulldozer did when he snored, so she led the girls into the coal-cellar. From there she found her way past the old cider press, then through the potato cellar, up into the courtyard. The five girls were nervous as they felt their way along the darkened, unfamiliar corridors. Their breaths came in short, sharp bursts as they tried not to let their teeth chatter. Finally they clambered over a cannon that was hundreds of years old, and managed to wriggle their way through a cellar window into the central courtyard. The six of them stood and listened for a moment. Everything was deathly silent.

Just as they were beginning to relax, Renate made a high-pitched squeak that she only just managed to catch before it turned into a scream. Everyone turned to see what had frightened her. In front of the castle wall, lit by the moon's weak light, stood a huge octopus-shaped monster. Closer inspection revealed it to be the fire pump, its hoses tangled up and sticking out in every direction.

No one wanted to admit that they had all been frightened by the 'octopus', so they all kept quiet. Then Sonya whispered, 'In case we lose each other, we go back to the lake the way we came: through this cellar window and turn left, over the cannon, along the corridors and we'll meet up at the canoes. Is that clear?'

The girls nodded.

'Then let's get going.'

Sonya turned and headed towards the entrance above the main staircase, which she knew was left open, even at night. The Shiverstone boys would have had taken great delight in the skill with which the girls carried out their practical joke – if only it hadn't been played on them!

Like seasoned burglars the girls climbed up the steps, keeping to the right of the banisters, where Sonya had told them the staircase wouldn't creak. The passageway was lit by a single night-light, pale as a dying glow-worm. It was as silent as a morgue. You couldn't hear even a single knight's snore.

From here on in the girls had agreed to communicate using only sign language. Sonya gestured for them to follow her. She snuck along the corridor and around the corner until she reached the end.

Shiverstone Castle had originally been designed for knights to live in, not schoolboys. It was four boys to each room, so even though the rooms were quite big, there was only enough room for each of them to have one bed and one small chest of drawers. The small chest of drawers was used by most of the boys to keep their socks, T-shirts and underpants in. The rest of their clothes and belongings were kept in the cupboards that lined the corridors outside their rooms. Sonya knew this because she had visited Shiverstone many times. It was her description of this arrangement one night when she was talking with Beatrix and Ingrid that had given the two girls the idea for their prank.

At the end of the corridor Sonya carefully opened the last cupboard on the right. She cautiously took out the contents – first the spare sheets, then the pants, jackets, jumpers, shirts and shoes, leaving only a few pages of piano music. It was Strehlau's cupboard.

Eva and Renate carried the clothes to the top of the staircase while Sonya, Beatrix and Ingrid started on all the other cupboards. Sophie, carrying the long rope, kept a lookout, listening for any suspicious sounds.

The mountain of clothes at the top of the stairs grew larger and larger. In no time it was huge. Once the cupboards on the first floor were empty, the girls started work on the second floor. Everything was going smoothly. Perhaps *too* smoothly.

The girls began to feel more confident. They started talking to each other in hurried whispers and started to muck around. Ingrid held up a particularly large shirt – belonging to Bulldozer – and mimicked one of her teachers. The others could barely hold back their laughter. The nervousness they'd felt when they'd arrived had completely disappeared.

Beatrix was just opening her twentieth cupboard when she saw something that immediately caught her attention. An electric guitar was resting against the corner of the cupboard under where the shirts were hanging. Beatrix knew from what Sonya had told her that there was only one guitarist in the castle. Her personal enemy, Steven. She was about to take it out when

Sonya came up behind her and tapped her on the shoulder. Beatrix turned around and Sonya shook her head, pointing at the clothes.

Beatrix closed the cupboard door, frustrated at the missed opportunity to get even with her enemy. From that moment on she lost interest in stealing the boys' clothes. The thought of getting her revenge for being called a 'witch' took over. She racked her brains trying to figure out how to get her hands on that guitar. She could already see Steven in her mind's eye, opening his cupboard next morning to find that not only were his clothes missing, but his beloved musical instrument was gone as well. Beatrix was determined to give him the shock of his life.

All the cupboards were empty and the girls began carrying the clothes out into the courtyard. Beatrix took the opportunity to hide from the others. She waited until everyone else was loaded up with an armful of clothes and heading downstairs, then looked around quickly, and scampered back to the second floor. Once she got there she stopped again and listened. No one downstairs seemed to be coming up after her. She tip-toed along the corridor until she reached the seventh cupboard.

It's a nice-looking guitar, she thought to herself as she opened the cupboard door. Filled with curiosity and excitement, she completely forgot about being careful. She reached for the instrument whose owner was not more than four metres away, sleeping the deep sleep of a growing knight. As a matter of fact, Steven wasn't sleeping very deeply at all. The embarrassment of the current situation, the consequences of which were made worse by Bulldozer's gossiping and teasing, combined with the memory of Beatrix's thankless reaction to his knightly confession all rumbled around in Steven's mind, preventing him from properly falling asleep.

In her haste and excitement Beatrix grabbed at the guitar too quickly. She knocked it against the side of the cupboard and the strings rang out in protest!

Hey! thought Steven, still half-asleep. That's my guitar! Like lightning he sprang out of bed and groped his way to the door. He figured that Bulldozer was trying some new prank, so he tensed his muscles, ready to tackle the muscle-mountain.

Steven carefully opened the door and peeked into the hall. He saw a figure holding up his guitar. With a panther's speed he leapt forward and grabbed hold of the thief and pushed him against the wall. But when Steven's hand grabbed for his opponent's neck, he realized it couldn't belong to Bulldozer. This neck was far too slender to be Bulldozer's! It was even too narrow to be Claus or Mosquito's. It couldn't be Strehlau he had pinned to the floor – Strehlau would never go near Steven's guitar without asking first. So who did he have here? Suddenly his struggling opponent let out a quiet grumble. By this time Steven's eyes had accustomed themselves to the darkness of the corridor, but he still didn't believe what he saw, and leaned in closer to get a good look at the thief's face. It was a girl! And not just any girl, it was Beatrix! Seeing her again made Steven furious.

'How did *you* get here?' he hissed at her.

'Ow! Let go! You're hurting me!' Beatrix said, giving a strangled gasp.

Steven had never fought a girl, and had no idea what he should do. He took his hand from her neck and held her against the wall by the shoulders while he thought. What should he do? Should he wake the others? No way! He had to find his own solution to this problem.

'Will you stop that!' he hissed at Beatrix, who had bitten him on the hand. She was desperate. She had to get out of here – but how? Where could she run to? Maybe through the creaking castle gate? What if she fought back? What would happen if she screamed?

Steven was also deep in thought. He had to buy some time. He needed to think things through and then act. He grabbed Beatrix by the arm and pushed her into his own cupboard, closing the door and turning the key.

He picked up his guitar and carried it into his room, then pulled his track suit over his pyjamas and pulled on a pair of gym shoes. Then he went out into the hallway, opened the cupboard door again, took hold of Beatrix before she could say anything, twisted one arm around behind her back and marched her ahead of him.

'If you scream or call out I'll lock you in the torture chamber,' he said, hoping that he could frighten her into being quiet. When they reached the stairs, Beatrix dug her heels in and refused to walk any further.

'I'll tell you what I was doing if you let go of my arm,' she whispered.

'If I let go you'll run away,' Steven whispered back. 'No, you're coming with me!' And with that he dragged her into the small room beneath the stairs that led to the attic. He and Otto had turned the room into a headquarters where they could plan their pranks and schemes. It was a well-equipped headquarters. There were torches, a portable heater, a kettle, instant soups and teabags, biscuits, ropes, skeleton keys and even a set of handcuffs. An old radio stood against the far wall. Steven switched on the light and locked the door behind him.

'So. Now you talk. Sit down.'

Beatrix sat down, rubbing her arm. For a moment they both sat staring at each other silently.

Funny, thought Steven, I've been thinking about this girl non-stop for the last week and suddenly here she is, in the middle of the night, trying to steal my guitar! Start with the facts, he thought, and broke the silence.

'You wanted to steal my guitar.'

Beatrix shook her head.

'Don't lie, I saw you.'

'You didn't see anything.'

'How did you get here?'

'How do you think?' she replied snippily.

'Did you come over here in a canoe?' he asked, surprised.

'Maybe,' she replied and shrugged her shoulders.

Steven wasn't learning anything from her this way. He fell silent and became thoughtful. Then he tried a

54

different tactic. Slowly and calmly he asked her, 'Why are you so mad at me? We dobbed ourselves in to your principal to save you.'

They looked at each other for a moment, then Beatrix hissed. 'Because of your stupid prank Ingrid and I had to peel potatoes for four days! You could have dobbed yourself in earlier, you coward!'

Now it was Steven's turn to explode. 'Take that back! I am not a coward, you . . . you witch!'

'Don't you *ever* call me that again!' she screamed, so loudly that Steven reached out to put his hand in front of her mouth. Beatrix did quieten down, but it was only because she was biting his hand again.

Steven snatched his hand back. 'Ow! Quit it! If you don't keep quiet I'll have to handcuff you!' he threatened.

'You're such a bully! You think you're so smart and so much stronger than me!' she spat back at him.

'Well, I am!' Steven said, giving as good as he got.

There's no talking to this girl, he thought. She's just making me mad, and that just makes her even madder. Then something occurred to him.

'How did you know it was my cupboard?'

Beatrix shrugged her shoulders again and wouldn't reply. Her thoughts were with her friends. They were probably finished by now, she thought, waiting for her down at the jetty. She had to get away from Steven!

Steven had decided that he would keep trying to get her to talk. 'Will you answer me?' he asked, grabbing hold of her wrist.

They looked at each other with hate-filled eyes.

Steven could feel the beat of Beatrix's pulse in her slender wrist. He loosened his grip. Suddenly Beatrix's expression changed, and Steven noticed she had green eyes.

'I just wanted to see how it played. I've only ever played acoustic before,' she said softly.

Steven was stunned. It was the last thing he'd expected. 'What?' he stuttered, still holding her by the wrist. 'You play guitar too . . .?'

Beatrix carefully pulled her arm away and Steven let go of her wrist. She kept looking at him, and then she nodded and began to laugh. Steven started laughing too. The tension in the air disappeared. It didn't feel like they were enemies any more.

'How long have you been playing?' Beatrix asked.

'I've been learning for four years,' said Steven proudly.

'I've only been playing for two,' said Beatrix, and they began to laugh again.

'Why are you laughing?' Steven asked.

'Because you are,' Beatrix replied.

'This is crazy! Here I was, thinking you were a real battle-axe . . .'

'And now?'

'Now I find out you're a guitarist too. Hey! We should jam together some time!'

'I don't think I'd play as well as you,' said Beatrix, shaking her head.

'How do you know?'

'I just don't think I would. You've been playing for twice as long as me.'

Steven wasn't convinced. But there was something that he liked about this girl. He decided to try being friendly towards her. Being angry certainly wasn't working.

'You know what?' he said, smiling. 'I'll go and get my guitar now. Maybe you can show me what kind of music you can play.'

'Okay,' Beatrix said, smiling back. 'That'd be great. I'll wait right here.'

But when Steven returned with his guitar under his arm, Beatrix was gone. At first he couldn't believe it, and looked for her outside. But she was nowhere to be found.

'That tricky monkey!' he said to himself.

In the meantime, the monkey was crawling through the coal cellar towards freedom as fast as she could go.

'Where were you?' asked Renate and Eva when she got back to the lake. Their teeth chattered with the cold. The first canoe had already departed, so that Sonya could prepare for the possibility that Beatrix had been caught.

'I heard a noise and had to hide,' she said as she crawled into the canoe. She didn't say another word for the rest of the trip home.

She was like a ghost, Steven thought as he crawled back to bed, glad that no one else had noticed anything. It's like she was never here. The tension he had felt over the last few days was gone. Feeling strangely light-headed, even happy in a weird sort of way, Steven rolled himself into a little ball, but he found it hard to sleep.

She's back on the other shore by now, he thought to himself as the sound of heavy rain began rattling on the roof. He finally fell asleep to the rhythm of the steady downpour.

Steven Declares His Colours

Strehlau was the first to notice that something was wrong. This week it was his turn to be on wake-up duty. He had to get up earlier than the others and knock on everyone's door to wake them. Still half-asleep, he groped his way to his cupboard to get into his tracksuit for the daily cross-country run. But when he opened the door, all he found was the sheet music that the girls had left behind. Because he was the brainiest student in the school he always assumed that people had it in for him, so he just thought someone was playing a joke. He decided to act like nothing was wrong, so he went back to his room and put on his dressing gown, then carried on with the wake-up duty. 'Time to get up!' he called, knocking on each door as he passed.

Soon there were lots of grumpy and half asleep knights standing in front of their cupboards, staring at . . . well, staring at nothing! Steven and Otto were no exception, which was lucky for them. When things like this happened in Shiverstone, people usually assumed it was something that Steven and Otto had planned. Bulldozer walked over to their cupboards just to check if they had 'conveniently' been skipped by the pranksters. When he saw that their cupboards were as empty as his, he seemed satisfied that they were not the guilty party and went back to his own cupboard.

That little monkey! thought Steven. He immediately worked out what had happened – Beatrix certainly hadn't been alone! He had to admit that he was impressed by the prank. Otto stood next to Steven, suspiciously watching all of the different expressions on his friend's face. He looked at Steven with his eyebrows raised, expecting an explanation.

'I'll tell you later,' said Steven.

'You'd better,' Otto growled back, unimpressed at his cupboard's emptiness.

The boys wandered down to the courtyard, expecting that they'd have to do the cross-country run in their pyjamas.

'Hey! Look up there!' called Mosquito. He pointed upwards and stared. Everyone looked at where he was pointing. Strung diagonally across the courtyard, from one wall to the other, was a long piece of rope on which item after item of clothing flapped like a giant load of washing.

'I'll be a monkey's uncle!' fumed Steven. 'How did they get up there?' Looking around the courtyard, he noticed the block and tackle that usually hung against the third post, now neatly leaning against the staircase banister, and his admiration for the girls grew.

61

'I don't believe it!' yelled Bulldozer suddenly. He was standing underneath the rope, jumping up and trying to get at his clothing. 'Our stuff's all wet!'

The clothes were dripping slow, steady drips of fresh morning dew down into the courtyard. Nobody was pleased at the discovery. Everyone looked at everyone else suspiciously.

Rex was astonished when he arrived at breakfast. His pupils stood at their chairs still in their pyjamas and dressing gowns, waiting for him to be seated. Mister Waldmann, who seemed to have an inkling of the reason for their strange appearance, pointed out the window. Rex looked outside. He hid his amusement with a stern shake of his head.

'Fair enough, you can stay dressed as you are for now. At least until the sun comes out,' was all he said before he sat down to eat his breakfast.

'He thinks it's funny,' growled Bulldozer, stuffing a big spoonful of cornflakes into his mouth.

'Why shouldn't he?' replied Mosquito. 'Nothing was broken or stolen, was it?'

If a visitor to the school had attended one of the classes that morning, they would immediately have run to the Minister for Education, to demand the closure of this bizarre school. The boys did look strange. The knights who often weren't very awake during class looked even more asleep than usual because of their pyjamas.

Everyone had a grumpy face as they tried to work out who had done this to them. They'd all decided that the only people who could have pulled this prank were the teachers. Mister Waldmann had already tricked one particularly lazy class into studying really hard for their exams by bringing in the Minister for Education's advisor to lecture them about the importance of a good education, and to scare them with horror stories about boys who failed their exams. After a week of this the class had been really well prepared – everyone passed brilliantly. The day after the exams Mister Waldmann revealed to them that the 'advisor' they were all so scared of was none other than Heini, the castle's chef, wearing a fake beard!

Mister Waldmann had earned himself a reputation for pranks after that episode. Seeing every student's clothing hanging on a long rope, it seemed obvious that Mister Waldmann was responsible for this latest mischief.

Relationships between teachers and students that day were tense. When teachers asked them a question, the boys' replies were short, sharp and to the point. They didn't talk to the teachers at all outside class. The teachers noticed, of course, but they seemed to think that the way the boys were behaving was funny, which only strengthened the case against them. And so the day ended with a brooding atmosphere, which wasn't helped by the fact that it had rained in the afternoon, wetting all the clothes once again.

One thing was clear. That night all the knights would get together and plan their revenge. When the younger pupils were in bed, the knights met for an extraordinary evening meeting in the torture chamber, the secret sanctuary where they held their knightly meetings.

Bulldozer, as chair of the meeting, stood behind the long stone table. He was so mad at the teachers that he wasn't thinking very clearly, so his speech was long and repetitive and boring. The boys let him talk, and made their own plans as he droned on and on. Steven was carefully watching Mosquito, who was sitting beside Bulldozer. His fingers drummed a restless beat against the tabletop.

Steven nudged Otto. He'd filled Otto in about the previous night's goings-on after breakfast. 'Check out Mosquito. He's up to something.'

Otto grumbled in reply. He was cross with Steven because he hadn't woken him, to help deal with Beatrix.

Finally Bulldozer's speech finished. Everyone breathed a sigh of relief. Next it was Mosquito's turn. He stood up and began to speak.

'Some people suspect the culprits of last night's prank are our teachers. But I'm not so sure. What do you think of this?' So saying he reached into his dress-ing-gown pocket and pulled out a hair-clip. Everyone stared wide-eyed at the object. It was clear evidence that *girls* had been responsible for the prank!

Mosquito cast a poisonous look in Steven and Otto's direction, adding, 'I found this in Steven's cupboard this afternoon.'

A loud murmur went around the room. Hans, who was taking minutes, had to ask for silence.

With a malicious grin, Bulldozer turned to Steven. 'Maybe you would be so good as to tell us where this comes from,' he said.

Steven's brain began working at a feverish pace. What should he do? There was no doubt that he was indirectly responsible for what had happened. *If only I hadn't apologised to Principal Horn*, he thought to himself. But then Beatrix would still be peeling potatoes! *Why has everything gone so pear-shaped?* he moaned to himself. He had behaved like a knight by admitting his responsibility for barricading the classrooms at Rose Cliffs. Doing the right thing had just got him and Otto into even *more* trouble!

Suddenly he had an idea. Had he really admitted to everything? No, he hadn't! The fear of being laughed at was the reason he'd kept the prank at Rose Cliffs secret. But everyone was laughing at him and Otto anyway. So what did he have to lose by telling everyone the entire truth? Nothing! It was clear that the truth was the only way out. He thought back to when he first arrived at Shiverstone. They'd all teased him mercilessly, but he'd hung in there and proven himself by saving the school, even though it had been really hard at times. What was happening now was nowhere near as hard as what he had already been through.

'We're waiting,' said Bulldozer, interrupting Steven's train of thought.

'I found a girl in the corridor this morning,' Steven said in a firm voice.

'Why didn't you tell us straight away?' Mosquito asked in a cutting voice.

'Because I thought she was only trying to steal my guitar.'

65

Steven told the knights the whole story. He told them that he had had no idea about the girls' plot to steal everyone's clothes. He told them that he'd assumed that Beatrix had come alone. But that didn't make his own situation any better.

'Well, then, everything comes down to you two, doesn't it?' said Mosquito. 'You took it upon yourselves to paddle over and admit to barricading the classrooms, and that's why those girls came here, and now none of us have a thing to wear.'

'Drinking tea with Waldmann in the evening – great knights you are,' said Bulldozer sarcastically, showing how unimpressed he was.

It was obvious to Steven and Otto that the real reason everyone was so annoyed with them was the special treatment they had received from Mister Waldmann and Rex.

'We're sorry about what's happened,' said Otto, springing to his friend's defence. 'We'll fix things. We promise.'

'That's the least we expect of you,' rumbled Bulldozer. He was still mad at Steven for making fun of him at the fire drill.

He's a muscle-mountain alright, but he's incredibly thin-skinned, thought Steven.

After a short discussion, Hans read out the following unanimous decision:

Steven and Otto have embarrassed the entire school, due to their egotistical actions. They have promised to come up with a suggestion to redress this shame within ten days.

If they do not find a solution in ten days our knights'
assembly will meet to decide upon a suitable punishment.
This meeting will remain a secret.

And with that, the meeting was over.

'I'm never going to play another prank again,' said
Otto as they left the torture chamber.

'It's a little late for that,' replied Steven. 'Now you
definitely *have* to play another one.'

Saving Honour

Steven was convinced that telling the truth at the meeting had been the right thing to do. The next day, everyone still seemed upset with him and Otto, but at least they had stopped teasing them about the girls' school.

Steven had learned his lesson. He was thinking it over that afternoon while they were building the hide. He sawed and hammered like crazy and behaved as though Otto wasn't even there. When Otto asked him a question he gave only short answers and then went back to thinking.

Otto wanted to talk about what they should do next. Ten days wasn't a very long time. He was worried about the 'suitable punishment' the knights were planning if he and Steven failed. But as soon as Otto started to say anything, Steven cut him off.

'Leave me alone. I don't care about that at all.'

There was definitely something big on Steven's mind. Something that he didn't want to talk about. But if you can't talk to your best friend about what's on your mind, what does that say about your friendship? Otto was starting to get annoyed.

Steven wasn't only like that with Otto. In class it was like he was on another planet. He was nervous and agitated. He scribbled a lot into a notepad he had hidden under his desk. Otto peeked at it between classes one day. It was sheet music! He's completely nuts! Otto said to himself. I'm going bonkers trying to come up with a prank for Rose Cliffs and he's writing a new song!

On the third day the two boys still hadn't talked about what they were going to do next. Otto decided to act more forcefully. When they paddled across the lake to start work on the hide, he turned to face Steven.

'We can't keep going on like this,' he said. 'We have to talk about what we're going to do.'

'No one's stopping you,' said Steven.

Otto lost his temper. 'What the hell is wrong with you? This is as much your problem as it is mine!'

Steven didn't say anything. For a while they paddled in silence, and then Otto tried again.

'Are you going to say *anything*?'

'Why don't *you* think of something?' Steven finally replied. 'You usually come up with good ideas. Me – I'm blank!'

They arrived at the stone pyramid, and Otto jumped out of the canoe. He started pulling it onto the shore. In silence the two walked over to the hide, not looking at or talking to each other. All of a sudden Steven started to whistle. Otto stopped what he was doing and stared at him, stunned.

'What are you looking at?' asked Steven.

'You're whistling.'

'Aren't I allowed to?'

'You've hardly been in a whistling mood over the last few days. It's just a surprise, that's all.'

Steven said nothing as he began to bang nails into the floor of the hide. Otto watched him suspiciously from out of the corner of his eye.

'If I'm not mistaken, you're behaving exactly like you've just had a really good idea,' he said after a while.

'I have,' replied Steven, without turning around. 'And it's about time, too. I've been racking my brains for days without coming up with a single decent idea. I was beginning to lose faith in myself!'

'That could never happen,' said Otto, still annoyed.

On the fifth day the animal hide was finished. Chainsaw and Rex were ceremonially paddled across the lake to view it.

All Rex had told the Count was that the boys had prepared a surprise for him to apologise for the unhappy outcome of the fire drill. The reminder of the embarrassment and damage made Chainsaw wear a severe expression on his face the whole way across the lake. But he was so curious about the surprise that he found it hard to maintain his stern expression. He managed to keep it in place until he saw the hide.

'This was surely made . . . hrrr . . . hrrrrrr . . . by a professional!' He didn't want to believe that two boys could pick such a perfect position for a hide. He imme-diately began to talk about 'his' school, and how proud he was of 'his' boys. And then he made an announcement that came as a complete surprise.

'In thanks . . . hrrrr . . . hrrrr . . . for this beautiful hide, I'd like to donate the fire pump to the school . . . hrrrr . . . for its exclusive . . . hrrrumph . . . use. And I'd . . . hrrrrr . . . hrrr . . . hrrumph . . . like to put these two lads . . . hrrrr . . . hrrr . . . in charge of it . . . hrrrr . . . permanently!'

The peace between Chainsaw and the school had finally been restored. But there was no time for Otto and Steven to waste. They only had five days left to avoid punishment from the rest of the knights. That evening after dinner, they visited Mister Waldmann's office.

'It's funny, you know,' said their teacher suddenly. 'Sonya hasn't called for a long time.'

'Interesting,' murmured Steven. 'But I can understand why.'

'You can?' asked Mister Waldmann.

'She's got a guilty conscience,' said Steven. 'The stolen clothes prank has Sonya's name all over it.'

'How do you figure?' asked Mister Waldmann, frowning.

'It's obvious. Those girls could never have found their way around here. It's all unfamiliar territory. Someone had to have shown them where to come.'

Even though they didn't want to believe that Sonya could turn against them, they had to admit it made sense. After they got over their initial disappointment, they decided they couldn't stay mad at her forever. She was a teacher at Rose Cliffs, after all, so of course she would side with the girls.

71

'Well, since Sonya tricked us we have every right to wreak our own revenge!' said Steven, his voice taking on the hardened air of a master criminal.

Mister Waldmann and Otto agreed. And they loved the plan he'd come up with. They put it into practice immediately.

Despite the late hour, Mister Waldmann made a call to the Rose Cliffs school. An unfriendly voice answered the phone and asked who would dare ring at this hour. Mister Waldmann gave his name and apologised politely, admitting that he was worried because he hadn't heard from his daughter for several days. The voice on the other end grew a little friendlier.

'Just a moment please, I'll have her paged.'

Finally Sonya came to the phone. Mister Waldmann continued to play the worried father. He switched his phone over to hands-free so that Sonya's voice came through the speaker loud enough for Otto and Steven to hear.

'Are you all right, Sonya?' he asked in a tremulous voice. 'I haven't heard from you for ages.'

'Oh Dad, I have so much work, it's all so new to me. It's taking so much time to get everything done. I haven't had time to call,' his daughter replied.

After making some small talk, Mister Waldmann began to lay his trap.

'Are your students very friendly?' he asked. 'Do you get along with them?'

'Oh yes!' she answered. 'And I get on really well with the two wildest girls. All the other teachers are scared of them, but they don't give me any problems.'

Steven and Otto rubbed their hands in glee. They had no doubt now that Sonya had been involved in the plot against them. Mister Waldmann nodded his head, preparing for the final volley.

'Steven and Otto asked me to say hello to you, by the way.'

'Did they?' Sonya replied after a moment's hesitation. 'How are they?'

'They were with me just a minute ago,' said her father. 'There's a hell of a mess going on over here.' He told her about the prank, and how whoever had done it had not been found out. 'In fact, the boys think we teachers did it!' he finished. Sonya promptly burst out laughing. In Otto and Steven's minds, her laughter was the last piece of evidence they needed.

Mister Waldmann turned the conversation to other matters. He would have made an excellent private investigator. He carefully asked her when she thought she might come and visit again. Maybe he could help her with her work somehow.

'That's very generous, Dad, but afternoons I have to supervise the girls at swimming.'

'Why don't you come here with the girls on Friday?' Mister Waldmann suggested. 'The rest of the school is going on an excursion to the Ringelback Power Station, so we'd have the place to ourselves.'

Sonya still wasn't convinced. But then Mister Waldmann told her about the bay right outside Shiverstone. There was more direct sunlight on the Shiverstone side than the bay at Rose Cliffs. Plus, the Shiverstone bay was straighter, deeper and longer. He could telephone

Principal Horn and check with her to see if it would be okay.

Steven and Otto's shoulders shook in silent mirth. Their teacher was in top form.

Sonya was seriously considering her father's offer. Finally the chance to show the girls the scene of the crime during daylight hours won her over. She said yes.

'All right. Friday afternoon. I'll expect you around four,' said Mister Waldmann before hanging up.

'This'll be the joke of the century!' Otto cheered. 'Just watch out – Bulldozer will burst with envy!'

'Mister Waldmann, you're worth your weight in gold!' added Steven, but the older man waved him off.

'You flatter me. Just make sure that my part in this is never mentioned.'

Surprised, Steven and Otto looked at him.

'Why not?' asked Otto.

'Because the others will think I'm playing favourites, and you'll be worse off for it.'

'That's not true!' Steven disagreed. 'Those guys need to know what a good guy you are!'

Next, Rex was brought in on the plan. Steven outlined the plan in point form, without elaboration. Rex listened and didn't interrupt, though he laughed out loud several times.

'I can see,' he said after Steven had finished, 'that you're not going to take this lying down. But I ask one thing. Whatever you do, please do the right thing and remain the knights you are. If you promise me no one will get hurt and that you won't be too rough, I'll turn a blind eye.' And with a final smile he added, 'You manage all that and I'll straighten things out with Principal Horn.'

Steven and Otto went looking for Bulldozer, so that they could tell the knights about their plan.

'I feel like a politician today,' said Otto. 'First we officially open the hide, then there's a cabinet meeting, with secret talks, and now a full assembly of parliament.'

Steven was back to being his old self again. He pitched the idea for the prank with such enthusiasm and force that even Bulldozer, who had opened the meeting with a face as dark as a thunder cloud, couldn't disagree with it. By the time Steven had finished explaining things, everyone agreed it was the practical joke of the millennium!

All the bad feelings were forgotten. The knights were overjoyed that Steven and Otto had provided them with the opportunity to become involved in such a fantastic practical joke. There was so much to organise that the assembly decided to meet again the following evening to talk about who would take care of what.

The night after the second meeting everyone went to bed and dreamed about the most fantastic plots and ideas.

75

Once Upon a Time in Salamis

Sonya told the girls that the Shiverstone boys still hadn't worked out who the culprits were. She went on to explain that the boys suspected their own teachers, at which point Beatrix began to jump up and down on the spot with excitement. Their own principal had no idea what had been going on, the boys were still in the dark, and now they had been given the opportunity to visit the scene of the crime in broad daylight! Maybe they'd even get the chance to play another practical joke! It was just too good to be true!

Because they were all in such great spirits, no one suspected that the invitation might be a trap. The only thing Beatrix thought was it was a pity the opposing school was going on an excursion on Friday. Otherwise she would have taken her guitar. As it was, the guitar remained at home, which was a lucky thing, as it turned out. That guitar's life was lengthened by years through the simple act of leaving it behind.

Sonya was the best swimmer of all the Rose Cliffs teachers, and had been given the job of looking after the girls when they were swimming. The younger girls had their lessons in the small bay outside the school, and later in the day it was the older girls' turn.

It was already autumn, and the bay was covered in shadows during the afternoon. The sun was not as warm at that time of day, so Sonya had asked for permission to take the canoes to a sunnier part of the lake. Where this sunnier part was, of course, she didn't say.

At about four o'clock, the girls set off. There were twenty of them in four canoes. Two girls sat in the back, two sat in the middle and paddled, and one sat right at the front. The lake was as smooth as a sheet of glass. Ahead of them Shiverstone Castle lay invitingly, soaking up the autumn sunshine. There wasn't a soul in sight, except for one familiar figure waiting for them on the jetty. It was Mister Waldmann. He waved to them as soon as he saw them. In the excitement there was one thing that the girls failed to notice. Unlike the night they had paddled across to play the prank, today there wasn't a single canoe in sight. Even though Beatrix and Ingrid had a lot in common with Steven and Otto, they missed this vital clue. They didn't have any idea that they might be paddling into a trap. They only saw Mister Waldmann waving at them, so they cheerfully, trustingly, paddled towards him.

The disappearance of the canoes could be put down to Steven remembering something from his history class. The sea battle that had taken place at Salamis in 480 BC, which Mister Waldmann had taught them about a few weeks earlier, had been on Steven's mind for a long time. He couldn't get the story of the Greek hero Themistocles, who had led the Greek navy to victory in that famous sea battle, out of his head. He decided that, in honour of the ancient sailor, the knights would involve the girls in a similar kind of sea battle.

Otto had immediately overtaken the technical side of the preparations. The knights had eight canoes at their disposal. Six of them were immediately set up for battle. They were camouflaged with branches and weeds so that when they were launched, their approach from across the lake would be disguised until it was too late for the girls to do anything about it. The other two boats were remodelled with planks and banisters, making a kind of floating bridge. On top of the platform the boys had mounted the present Chainsaw had bestowed upon the school in appreciation for his new hide: the water pump. The knights had built the only double-hulled battleship in naval history.

While the Rose Cliff girls paddled towards Mister Waldmann, the Shiverstone navy lay in wait, well-hidden and strategically placed to the right and left of the jetty, where the bushes grew down to the water. The destroyers, under Bulldozer's leadership, were ready to strike. Inside the boatshed, the double-hulled battleship had Admiral Steven Brewer on board.

'Here they come,' Mister Waldmann called, softly enough so that the girls couldn't hear him.

'Roger!' Steven called back softly. With Otto's help he gave the spray pump one final inspection. It all looked just right. Everything was in place. Otto was rubbing his hands in anticipation.

The girls were now within calling distance.

'Welcome to Shiverstone!' said Mister Waldmann, greeting them in order to distract them. The girls answered with an excited shout hello.

'Did you remember to bring your bathers?' he asked. The girls all called out 'Yes!' in unison.

That was the signal for Bulldozer's destroyers to launch themselves. Continuing to distract the girls, Mister Waldmann started to yodel. The girls giggled at the strange sight and began yodelling back, while those who weren't paddling fell about in helpless laughter.

The diversion worked brilliantly. The destroyers had been launched, but the girls hadn't noticed a thing. The camouflage was working perfectly.

'Are they in for a surprise,' Otto thought to himself as he peeked through the battleship's camouflage, watching the boats encircle the girls.

All of a sudden a shout of dismay lifted into the air. The girls had become aware of their predicament.

'I don't believe you could do this, Dad!' Sonya shouted at her father.

'I didn't believe you would pull a prank the way you did, either,' was her father's cool reply. He was smirking as he watched the action from the safety of the jetty.

Otto waited until the destroyers had completely surrounded the girls, cutting off all escape, until he opened the boatshed door.

'Okay boys, let's do it!' he shouted. 'Paddle as hard as you can!'

Ten of the younger boys began moving the heavy

battleship forward using long poles which they pushed into the bottom of the lake. Meanwhile, events outside were progressing to plan. The girls had been corralled into a small defenceless group. Their oars had tangled together and they could no longer free themselves to push off. Shouting angrily, their jeans already soaked, they huddled on their seats while the crews manning the destroyers, wearing only bathers, smacked the water with their oars, sending huge sprays over the enraged girls.

'Push! Push!' Steven called to the battleship's four paddlers, who puffed and panted like steam engines.

Sonya was the first to rally. She began giving orders to the girls. 'Let's get out of here!' she screamed, grabbing an oar. 'We need to split up!'

The girls began pushing the canoes apart with their oars.

'Look!' screamed one of them, pointing in the direction of the battleship. It was a frightening sight as it came towering towards them. The girls were hypnotised by the bizarre sight, and forgot that they were trying to escape.

'Now!' shouted Otto and began working the pump's lever like a madman.

'Anyone thirsty?' Mosquito called out. There was a gurgle and the first volley of water hit its goal, soaking all four boats with one shot. 'Bullseye!'

'Halt machinery,' Steven ordered, trying to sound like a naval captain. He was worried that if they got any closer and kept using the pump, they'd sink the girls' boats. The pump's water pressure was amazingly strong.

The girls, completely drenched by now, tried to get away. But it was too late. Their boats spun in circles as they tried to decide on a direction to move. As soon as one canoe managed to free itself from the rest, it was pushed back by the splashing and thumping of the destroyer battalion's oars.

'Want to see William Tell in action?' yelled Mosquito and aimed the hose at one girl's baseball cap, which was promptly removed from her head, landing metres away, next to one of the destroyers.

Suddenly one of the canoes broke free. Screaming like berserkers, the two girls in charge of the oars paddled like crazy towards the destroyers, trying to smash their way through.

'That's Beatrix!' Steven called out. 'All hands on deck!' But the heavy battleship couldn't move as quickly as the smaller canoe.

'Fill that old box,' Steven yelled at Mosquito, who immediately widened the pump's spray to arc up and over the trapped canoes and straight into the escapees' boat. The canoe began filling like a bathtub. By this time Bulldozer had noticed the escaping girls. In a few short strokes of the oar his destroyers were beside the canoe. What Bulldozer did next, Steven would never have given him credit for.

Disregarding the risk of being soaked himself, Bulldozer reached over and grabbed the oar out of Beatrix's hand. But she wasn't beaten. In a few short seconds she had grabbed the second oar and began paddling once more, moving shakily but surely out of the water cannon's reach. But Bulldozer hadn't given up. He was coming at her from the other side. It only took two swift moves, and the canoe was oarless, unable to escape.

'I suppose you think you're pretty special!' Beatrix screamed at him.

'That's it. They're finished,' Steven said, still pumping energetically.

'The most successful naval campaign since 480 BC,' grinned Otto from his position at the bottom of the pump's handle.

In the meantime Hans had taken the oars from another canoe. That left Sonya's canoe the only one capable of seriously resisting. She stood straight up in the middle of the boat and called out orders to the other girls.

'Careful Renate, behind you! More to the left, Sophie!'

Finally one of Mosquito's well-aimed salvos hit her squarely in the back, toppling her into the water. A wave of laughter from the jetty followed the well aimed squirt. Standing in a crowd, the rest of the Shiverstone students called encouragement to their seafaring heroes as though they were a football team playing a home game. Another of Mosquito's volleys sent a second girl into the water.

'Ha ha, I can swim!' she called out as soon as she surfaced.

Suddenly Steven felt something grab hold of his leg. He clung onto the pump and turned around. It was Beatrix! She must have dived under the battleship to get to him!

'Into the lake with you, you coward!' she yelled up at him, continuing to pull his leg.

'What do you mean coward?' Otto asked, turning around and trying to pry Beatrix's fingers from around Steven's ankle.

'There's no art in using superior firepower to win the upper hand,' she hissed back at him, letting go of Steven and treading water.

'It's not supposed to be an artform, it's payback!' Mosquito shouted, giving as good as he got.

Bulldozer muscled his way into the act, jumping from his destroyer onto the battleship. He grabbed an oar and used it to push Beatrix under the water.

'That's going too far!' said Steven. He tried to wrestle the oar away from Bulldozer while Beatrix resurfaced, gasping for air.

'You can't tell me what to do!' bellowed Bulldozer so loudly, that everyone looked at him. He wrapped his arms around Steven's middle so that the two boys were knotted together, tugging at the oar. As the battle raged towards the far end of the platform, something was bound to go wrong. The inevitable happened. In the confusion Beatrix grabbed the oar, wrestled it away from both of them, and pushed the two rivals out of the boat.

A big cheer went up on both sides. While the Admiral and his Commander-in-Chief continued to fight under water, the war up above came to an end.

'My shoe!' complained a girl whose soaked skirt clung to her legs like cling-wrap. A group of boys immediately disappeared under the waves, in a race to find Cinderella's lost slipper. In the meantime all of the other floating swimwear, hats, towels and sunglasses were gathered together. Oars were returned, and the girls took advantage of the gesture to push as many sailors over-board as they could. Sonya swam back to the jetty and handed her drowned wrist-watch up to her father.

'I deserve a new one for this!'

'And you'll get one, my child,' he replied in a friendly tone of voice. It seemed like a fair deal to him.

'I'll hold you to that,' she laughed as she swam back towards her canoe.

Steven and Bulldozer had also returned to their respective boats. Both of them had swallowed a lot of water.

Beatrix, the heroine of the day, swam back to her canoe and eagerly helped her friends to bucket the water back into the lake. Claus, the joker, paddled over and handed her a tiny jar the size of a thimble. 'This might come in handy,' he said.

The girls weren't annoyed at all. In fact, they had enjoyed splashing around with the boys. Waving and blowing mock air-kisses, they turned around to paddle home.

'Send our regards to Principal Horn!' Steven shouted out to them.

He could hear the girls laughing for a long time before they finally paddled out of hearing range.

The Leopards Change Their Spots

It wasn't possible to keep their excursion to Shiverstone a secret. The girls had thought of an ingenious plan to hide their soaked clothing – they changed into their bathers and returned home in those. The problem was that walking around the school in your bathers was against the rules of Rose Cliffs. The other problem was that their wet clothing left tell-tale drips all along the passageways. To top it off, the caretaker couldn't help noticing that every one of the canoes had been somehow filled with water. The game was well and truly up and no excuse helped. If Sonya had tried to blame the state of the girls and the canoes on horseplay or too much energy it would only have made things worse.

Eventually Ingrid finally worked up the courage to explain that whilst paddling past Shiverstone the boys had sprayed them with the school's fire pump.

Principal Horn immediately phoned Rex to complain. But Rex was prepared. He didn't hold back at all.

He hardly thought that what had happened could be described as a brutal attack. It sounded to him more like a carefully thought-out plan of action. In his opinion it was something the girls could think about in view of the recent episode involving the missing clothes at Shiverstone. This was the first that Principal Horn had heard of the girls' prank. She immediately sentenced the guilty parties to indefinite potato peeling duty.

The following day Principal Horn called Rex back. She'd had time to think things over and had found something else to complain about. Stealing the boys' clothing was, after all, nothing more than a retaliatory action that the girls had undertaken in return for the classrooms being locked up by two Shiverstone students. So if anyone was to blame, it was the Shiverstone boys.

The continuing argument between the two principals was followed with great interest by both students and teachers at both castles. It all came down to a battle between two separate ways of looking at the world. Everyone was fascinated to find out how it would end.

Rex seemed to be really enjoying sparring with Principal Horn. One afternoon he even paddled across the lake to have a private meeting with her. The secret spy network that existed between Sonya and Mister Waldmann worked exceptionally well, and had much to report. The boys were in the sports field doing athletics when Mister Waldmann arrived with the news.

'Rex and Principal Horn have just left the meeting room with smiling faces!'

Naturally the boys were waiting for Rex when he arrived back at the jetty, but he didn't say a word. He

87

preferred to leave them guessing. It wasn't until after dinner that he stood up and tapped his spoon against a glass to get their attention. When everyone had quietened down, he began his speech.

'Your sea battle has done me a huge favour, and I want to thank you. You've helped me convince Principal Horn that my teaching policies are appropriate for a rural school. I've explained to her how we all came to a decision to run the school not on punishment, but on trust. There's a freedom here as long as everyone takes full responsibility for their actions. She was astonished to hear how well it works.'

He paused and the teachers and students gave him a round of applause.

'In fact she was so surprised,' Rex continued, 'that she's decided to try our system over at her school.'

Now it was the boys' turn to be surprised. A murmur ran around the hall.

'I think the person who deserves special mention for this sudden reversal in Principal Horn's attitude is our much beloved Sonya Waldmann.'

This time everyone clapped at once. Mister Waldmann looked proud and embarrassed at the same time.

'And now,' Rex concluded, 'I have one more surprise in store for you. In order to keep the relationship between the two schools open and friendly, Principal Horn has invited us all over to her school for a garden party, next Saturday.'

An unbelievably loud cheer broke out. No one had expected that! Rex held up his hands to indicate he had something else he wanted to say.

'But if any of you embarrass me in any way at all next Saturday,' he said smiling sunnily, 'you'll be turning the sportsground into a potato field on Sunday!'

Being Forgiven ... with Music and Cake

There was seldom an event that so changed a school than the Rose Cliffs garden party changed Shiverstone. The teachers had to constantly confiscate combs and nail scissors during class. Mister Bach, the barber from Newtown, had to make a special visit to Shiverstone to take care of all the people who wanted to spruce up their looks.

But the knights' biggest worry was never openly talked about. Would the girls from Rose Cliffs want to dance? Instead of admitting that none of them had ever learned to dance properly, the knights crept away and stayed locked in their rooms and in empty classrooms, secretly practising made-up dance steps to melodies that they whistled under their breath. In the evenings leading up to the garden party, in the two hours between dinner and bedtime there wasn't a single room in the entire building where you couldn't hear a soft whistling coming from inside.

Bulldozer practised his dance steps with Mosquito in one of the classrooms. Mosquito led the dance.

Bulldozer was 'the lady', but that didn't stop him from treading on his partner's toes. It's no wonder Mosquito suddenly stopped midway through the dance and said, 'I've never met a girl as goofy-footed as you. I'd rather dance with a cupboard!'

Of course everyone heard about that one. Most of their own attempts at learning to dance had ended in similar disasters. Pretty soon everyone had started using the phrase 'pushing cupboards' instead of the word 'dancing'. Steven was nowhere near as worried as the other boys. Excalibur's band members didn't have to worry about dancing, because if there was going to be any dancing they'd be playing! In the lead up to the dance the five of them rehearsed like crazy and soon had a set-list that went for almost forty minutes.

Saturday finally arrived. By three o'clock the entire school was assembled in the courtyard with their bikes. No one had ever looked so clean before. Even Hans had swapped his usual checked shirt for a white one.

'Man, look at you!' Otto remarked to Werner, who had changed the way he looked most of all. His ratty, shaggy nest of hair was as shiny as an oiled sardine.

Werner's change of appearance confused little Herbert. 'Do we have to part our hair so that we can dance?' he asked.

Rex arrived, shaking his head as he looked from one boy to the next.

'If your exercise books were as neat as you look today, I'd be ecstatic!' he said. Then he jumped onto his bike. The whole school was ready to leave. There was no turning back now.

The girls had taken a lot of trouble to make everything as perfect as possible for their guests. In the large field in front of the castle they had set four poles into a huge rectangle. Strung across the poles were paper chains on which hung colourful paper mache flowers. At the far of the field stood a refreshment tent. At the closer end was a stage, with amplifiers and microphones ready to be set up. A piano stood at one side of the stage.

'You brought that for nothing,' said Steven, indicating Strehlau's keyboard, which was slung diagonally across his back in its travel case. Steven's guitar was similarly slung across his own back.

'Nah, this has a better sound,' said Strehlau.

The caretaker came out to meet the knights, and suggested that they lean their bikes against the trees at the edge of the forest. Then Principal Horn came out to meet them. She greeted Rex and introduced the teachers. Rex, in turn, introduced the Shiverstone teachers. Principal Horn then gave a short speech.

'My dear boys,' she began. 'Since your principal has told me so much about you – all good, I assure you – and as I've gleaned a bit more information through other means, I thought it was high time to get to know these perfect students personally!'

A happy murmur ran through the rows of boys. 'That Horn isn't so bad' mumbled Bulldozer.

Principal Horn continued. 'I therefore extend a hearty welcome to you, here at Rose Cliffs, and hope that you meet my expectations.'

Rex applauded. Everyone else joined in.

'Over there!' whispered Otto pointing across to the castle.

The girls were coming. Steven immediately recognised the girl on the left in the third row. It was Beatrix. They stopped at the small stage and waved to the boys.

Several girls moved onto the stage. Two were carrying violins. The third girl had a flute tucked under her arm.

'Isn't that Ingrid?' asked Steven.

'Where?' asked Otto.

'With the flute.'

'Is her name Ingrid?' Bulldozer turned around.

'Ingrid, Maria, Renate,' replied Mosquito, pointing to each of the girls in turn.

'How do you know?' Bulldozer asked, annoyed.

'Because Mum told me,' Mosquito answered back. 'That girl's my sister,' he said, pointing at Ingrid.

Suddenly Otto felt something dig into his ribs. 'Look at Beatrix,' said Steven, as she carried an acoustic guitar onto the stage.

'I'm looking. But that doesn't make me a punching bag,' muttered Otto.

Mrs Buckle, the plump teacher they'd met on the steps so many weeks ago took her place at the piano and the five of them began to play a sweet sounding song. The girls seemed extremely nervous. Ingrid played her flute so softly that it was almost impossible to hear her. Beatrix was also nervous. Steven immediately noticed when she played a wrong chord in the second verse.

Despite the girls' nerves, the performance was greeted with a huge round of applause. The knights clapped so loudly you'd think they were being paid. Bulldozer applauded loudest and longest. When he had finally settled down, it was time for a short intermission.

'Ladies and gentlemen, the evening continues over here,' a voice called to them from the refreshment tent. It was Sonya. She was immediately surrounded and greeted by a crowd of Shiverstone students.

'We should set up and play a warm-up,' said Steven to Otto, wanting to head to the stage, where Beatrix was still standing.

'Let's look after our stomachs first,' said Otto, heading towards the refreshment tent with Strehlau and Hans in tow.

Rolle, the sport's teacher arrived. 'Help me unload my bass,' he said, pulling Steven away from the stage. The two of them walked across to the bicycles, where Rolle had tied his instrument, tucked safely inside its hard case, to the sidecar of his motorcycle.

Both schools were hanging around in the refreshment tent, so Steven was able set up instruments without anyone noticing. Or helping. Finally Hans and Strehlau showed up, their mouths stuffed with cake. Only Otto was missing.

Steven jumped down off the stage and pushed his way through the throng until he finally found Beatrix.

'Hi,' he said.

'Hi,' she replied, but before they could say anything else a girl swooped in and pulled Beatrix away.

Otto was standing at the front of the tent, both his cheeks stuffed full. Steven gave him a small push.

'Come on, we're playing.'

Otto reached out for another sandwich.

'Get a move on! The kit's already set up.'

Tucking two more sandwiches into his jacket pocket, Otto trotted along behind Steven, a third sandwich in his mouth.

The band was a complete surprise to the Rose Cliffs girls. The first song they played was an up-tempo one to get everyone in the mood. Pretty soon there were two rows of girls lined up in front of the stage. They seemed to really like the music. Beatrix pushed her way to the front, pulling Ingrid along behind her. She stood there, looking up at Steven as he played.

Bulldozer, who usually had no interest whatsoever in music, was suddenly standing beside Ingrid, shaking his head to the beat and sneaking glances at Mosquito's sister. When the first number had finished, huge applause broke out.

Steven nodded to Otto and he tapped the rim of the snare to count the band in. The next song was more of a dancy number. The girls began to clap their hands along with the beat, but the boys were too nervous to ask anyone to dance. Steven saw that Bulldozer was already deep in conversation with Ingrid, and it gave him an idea. He held up his hand and stopped playing. The rest of the band followed his example. Everyone looked up at them, expecting a surprise.

Steven stepped up to his microphone. 'None of you fatigued knights seem to notice that the ladies want to dance,' he said. 'I therefore ask our two principals for permission to make the next dance a ladies' choice.'

That suggestion was taken up with great enthusiasm by the girls. Rex and Principal Horn nodded their approval. Several boys quickly disappeared into Sonya's refreshment tent.

The band started up again. Bulldozer was still so engrossed in his conversation with Ingrid that he hadn't been listening to a single word Steven had said. He was completely surprised when Ingrid grabbed his hand and dragged him onto the dance floor.

'Nice one,' grinned Otto from behind his drum kit.

Now Beatrix was the only one not dancing. She stood at the edge of the stage, looking from one band-member to the next. Suddenly she jumped up onto the stage and walked up to Steven.

'What are you up to?' he asked, still playing. The rest of the band watched with amused grins on their faces.

Beatrix reached out and pressed her hand against the guitar strings. There was an electrical screech as Steven stopped playing. The rest of the band kept going as though there was nothing the matter at all.

'I want to dance with you!' Beatrix said to Steven. 'You did say ladies' choice!' She lifted the guitar over Steven's head and dragged him off the stage.

'You dug your own grave,' Otto said scornfully. Hans started laughing so hard that he missed out on an entire verse. Only Rolle, Strehlau and Otto were able to continue playing.

Steven had no idea what hit him.

'I wish I could play like you do,' Beatrix said, stepping in close and putting her arms around Steven's shoulders.

Steven said nothing. He concentrated on dancing. The grass surface of the dance-floor helped a lot. It was so uneven that any bad step he made could be blamed on the grass.

Pretty soon the rest of the boys discovered the advantages of the rough ground as well. Bulldozer's dancing style seemed to involve jumping around like a boxer in the ring.

'Dancing is great for the calf muscles!' he called over to Steven and Beatrix as he jitterbugged past them with Ingrid in tow.

By this time Steven had gained enough confidence to be able to dance and talk at the same time.

'When are we going to jam together?' he asked

'Oh,' Beatrix said, trying to get out of it, 'I don't think I have time.'

'Why? You just played with the others.'

'I wouldn't really call it "playing",' she said, pulling a face.

Steven grinned. 'It was good – except you played G instead of F sharp!'

'Don't rub it in!' she growled and turned her back on him. Steven did the only thing he could think of. He ignored her pretend sulking and led her into the middle of the dance floor. He looked around and could see knights jogging up and down, disco dancing, waltzing, pogoing and twisting. One or two were even trying a kind of awkward tango, while Claus manoeuvred a short girl across the grass in his version of a quick-step. And in the centre of the dance floor, a little girl with plaits and a thick pair of glasses was dancing with Mister Waldmann!

'Will you look at that,' Steven said to Beatrix, and they burst out laughing. Then they continued to dance silently for a while.

'You know what?' Beatrix began again, abruptly. 'You should get back up on stage and play an honorary waltz for Rex and Principal Horn.'

'That's a good idea,' Steven agreed.

'Well, those two have certainly found one another,' a voice suddenly croaked behind them. Steven turned around to see that they'd arrived at the edge of the field, right in front of Principal Horn, who was watching the party with Rex. Feeling embarrassed, Steven and Beatrix danced in the opposite direction as unobtrusively as they could.

'Did you hear what she said?' Steven asked after a moment's pause.

Before Beatrix could answer, the music broke off, the piece had ended. The suddenly dance-obsessed knights clapped their approval loudly and shouted out for them to keep going, but Otto shook his head.

'I've got to get back,' said Steven, and letting go of Beatrix's hand he squeezed his way through the throng.

'Play that waltz,' she called after him. He nodded, jumped up on stage and said, 'Let's do that three-four number we rehearsed yesterday.'

Then he clapped his hands and waited until the audience had grown quiet.

'Could you please all form a circle?' he asked. 'That's right, a circle around Principal Horn and Principal Meyer. This next song is dedicated to our principals! If you know how to waltz, there's never been a better time!'

Enthusiastic calls rose up from the crowd. The girls and the knights linked hands and in less than a few seconds the two principals were surrounded.

'Alright!' Beatrix clapped loudly. Steven started the count-in. Rex waited for the music, expecting something with a fast pace like the rest of the music Excalibur had been playing. But when the *one-two-three, one-two-three* . . . rhythm began, he clasped the host school's principal around the waist and the two of them started to waltz so smoothly that everyone stared in amazement. Sonya had come out of the refreshment tent and stood beside her father, watching the two principals dance.

'What's going on?' she asked, shaking her head. 'Ever since Rex paid Principal Horn a visit she's had a complete change of personality.'

'The spirit of the ghosts of the knights of Shiver-stone is contagious,' said her father, his pride shining through, 'You've passed it on to this school, too.'

When the waltz had finished, Excalibur played another catchy pop tune and the knights and their girls started dancing again. The ice had been so thoroughly broken by now, and the atmosphere was so merry, that Steven didn't have to instigate ladies choice for the rest of the night.

The band took a break halfway through their set. Beatrix had been sitting on the corner of the stage through the entire bracket, listening with interest.

'Finally,' groaned Otto. 'I died of thirst half an hour ago!'

The band charged into the refreshment tent. Strehlau was just pouring himself a huge glass of lemonade when Mrs Buckle came up to him.

'You've got an unusual style of keyboard playing, young man,' she said softly. 'Would you mind if I sat in on the piano in the next bracket? I'd like to try playing a four-handed piece.'

'That doesn't sound like a bad idea,' Steven whispered to Beatrix. He grabbed his guitar and Beatrix grabbed hers and the two of them moved off to a bench near the castle's entrance.

'Do you know this one?' Steven asked, starting to play the first few chords of a song he'd heard on the radio the other day. Beatrix nodded and joined in. After a few goes they both found the rhythm and began matching each other's harmonies and melodies. Beatrix played the melody and Steven played the variations, counter-melodies and trickier finger movements.

'This is so much fun!' Beatrix said, smiling so brightly that her face shone.

Back on the dance floor, Claus had taken over as master of ceremonies. He had lined everyone up in two rows. The person at the start of each row was given a matchbox to balance on top of their nose. When Claus shouted 'Go!' they had to pass it on to the next person without anyone using their hands. Then that person had to do the same to the next person in line. If the matchbox fell, that row had to start all over again.

It was a lot of fun. Bulldozer stood behind Ingrid shaking with laughter, because she had so much trouble balancing the matchbox on his bulbous nose. It was just too big. In the other row, Mosquito had similar problems with Principal Horn's long, skinny nose. When, after the matchboxes had been dropped what seemed like hundreds of times, the row on the right eventually won.

By then Steven and Beatrix had returned with their guitars for one last fanfare.

The afternoon turned to evening, and when the knights finally thought about going home it was already starting to get dark. Principal Horn thanked them all for coming and suggested having another party soon. The girls waved goodbye until all the knights were out of sight.

On the way home Bulldozer rode beside Steven. 'Man,' he said, 'I used to wish that you had never come to Shiverstone, but your idea for the battle with Rose Cliffs – that was pure genius!'

'Yeah, it was.' Steven smiled at him cheekily. 'That Ingrid's not too bad, is she?'

Which made Bulldozer peddle off fast, his face red, while Steven's smile broadened as he thought about Beatrix.

About the author

Oliver Hassencamp (1921–1988) was 12 years old when he went to the Salem Castle boarding school on Lake Constance, Germany. Salem Castle was the inspiration for Shiverstone Castle, and while at school, Oliver – a talented musician who played saxophone, clarinet, trumpet and accordian – founded a jazz band which soon became renowned outside the school. On leaving school, he studied law, history of art and psychology before going to acting school. He worked as an actor, revue performer and writer in Munich, and later worked in film, radio and television. Since the first book about Shiverstone Castle was published in 1959, Oliver Hassencamp's much-loved series has been discovered by over a million enthusiastic readers.

Internet: www.schreckenstein.de

Editor's note

In translating the 'Burg Schreckenstein' (Shiverstone Castle) books from German to English, we have made every attempt to retain the original enthusiasm and affection the boys have for their teachers and their surroundings. On occasion, we have updated technical bits and pieces (such as sound systems), as well as moving the band out of jazz and into rock'n'roll. Once or twice we have made reference to people or events which would not have existed when the books were first written, in order to make the stories relevant to today's readers. We have also shortened a surname here or there, or simplified some place names, when these proved a touch difficult for young English readers to pronounce. And, like Oliver Hassencamp's millions of fans, we enjoyed the boys' adventures immensely once we discovered them. We hope you do too!